To Laura

Merry (
& a Happy New Year
but most importantly

... have a spooky
Valentine's Day!

Love you to Death

Leilanie Stewart
XO

4

Love you to Death
Ghost stories for Valentine's Day

Leilanie Stewart

Also by Leilanie Stewart

Belfast Ghosts Series

Book 1: The Blue Man

Book 2: The Fairy Lights

Book 3: Matthew's Twin

Other novels

The Buddha's Bone

Gods of Avalon Road

Short Story and Poetry Collections

Pseudologia Fantastica

Diabolical Dreamscapes

The Redundancy of Tautology

A Model Archaeologist

Toebirds & Woodlice

To JR and KJ, who love horror almost as much as I do.

Contents

1   White Day Whispers   1

2   Stone cold heart   53

3   Violets are blue   65

4   Cassandra's Call   91

5   A haunted Lupercalia   107

6   Brocken Spectre   127

7   Inamorata   152

8   Love you to Death   168

     Other books by Leilanie Stewart   194

     About the author   203

     Acknowledgements   205

1

White Day Whispers

"Did you know that in Japan, Valentine's Day isn't about *men* being romantic to women? It's a day when single *women* get a chance to let a guy know if they like him. She gives dark chocolates to the bloke she secretly fancies, and if he likes her too, he gives her white chocolate a month later on White Day on the fourteenth of March."

Carrie grinned. Her friend, Natalie, sure was full of interesting facts.

"And what if he doesn't like her?" Carrie asked.

"He gives her cookies as a rejection." Natalie shrugged. "Either way it's a win-win. She gets a treat no matter what."

Carrie sighed. "Wish we could do that custom over here. I'm sick of always being single and sad on Valentine's Day. Maybe I should take a leaf out of your book and go to teach English in Japan for a year. I hate how as soon as Christmas is over, all the shops over here get full of red hearts and teddy bears. It makes me want to puke."

Natalie scanned the bar over the top of her banana daiquiri. "What about that guy playing pool?"

Carrie glanced in the direction her friend looked. "He's a bit too good-looking. A bloke like that, who's too ripped, would be a magnet for women. I would worry he's cheating on me."

Natalie waved her concerns away with a flap of her hand. "Not all men are cheaters like Richard was."

Being reminded of her ex was the last thing Carrie wanted on Valentine's Day. She took a big swig of her gin and tonic and watched the sexy pool-player as he bent over to line up his cue. No harm in looking.

"You know what I think you need to do to get over Richard?"

Carrie peeled her eyes away from the man's muscular ass and turned to her friend.

"You need to get laid," Natalie continued, matter-of-factly.

She laughed. "Not everything is about sex. What about true love? What about fate? Why do other people get to fall in love with a bloke who's a keeper, and get married – but not me?"

Natalie puckered her lips. "I didn't know you were so sappy. I thought you hated hearts and teddies. You said Valentine's Day makes you want to puke."

"Only because I'm such a sad-sack loser that can't keep a guy." She gave a one-shouldered shrug, hoping it would come off as nonchalant.

"Come on, Carrie. I say it's about time you took a bit more control of your dating life."

"I've been trying." She shook her head. "It's not like I haven't been on dating apps and, whatever. I just haven't found anyone I like. There was Mr. Pervert who told me on our first date that actually he wasn't single, and that he and his partner were looking for a threesome, and then there was Mr. Psycho who had so much pent-up anger he actually squeezed his wine glass and broke it over his pasta carbonara."

Natalie gave a sympathetic smile over her banana daiquiri.

"I'm thirty-six and I'm single, and I feel like I'm on the shelf. My biological clock isn't ticking, it's like Big Ben booming in my ear," Carrie huffed.

Natalie's pitying look turned into laughter, spraying her with banana daiquiri. "Sorry, didn't mean to laugh. You have a way with words."

"You know, you're right though. Maybe I should be more proactive about finding a good guy for me. I really like this whole Japanese way of letting the ladies take the lead."

"Oh yeah?" Natalie leaned forward, cupping her chin in her palms. "Who have you got in mind for this little love-experiment, then?"

She took a deep inhale, allowing herself time to think. "There's this cute guy called Ken who moved into the flat above me. I think he just broke up with his girlfriend last night too. I heard them having a huge bust-up that went on all night. I heard her screaming at him and smashing stuff on the floor. She must've been psycho, poor guy."

Natalie raised one eyebrow. "I dunno, Carrie. A rebound thing doesn't sound like the best way to find true love."

She tossed her head. "I know. But I'm cautious. It might turn out to be a bit of fun for us both. You know, a harmless fling. Besides, I'm a totally different type from her. She was all, pink cheeks and black curly hair, whereas I'm so pale and redheaded. There's no way I'd remind him of her, so it would be a fresh start for him too, and it could be what I need to get my confidence back up in the whole dating scene. Do you want to know the weirdest coincidence? I think he might be Japanese. Or half-Japanese."

Natalie finished the rest of her banana daiquiri and licked the foam off her lip. "Interesting. Well, if you think it's a good idea, then I don't see the harm in it, I suppose. You've both come out of rocky relationships, so maybe a bit of fun would be the best thing for you both."

**

It was good of Natalie to come out for a drink with her on Valentine's Day, even if she couldn't help but feel like it was a pity drink. Carrie knew she was a hopeless romantic at heart; Natalie was a good friend – and a shoulder to cry on whenever she needed to pour out her broken relationship woes. She knew Nat was only doing it because her husband, Barry, worked late on weekday evenings, so she had free time. Still, even if it had been a pity drink, Nat owed her. She had been there for Nat during all her and Barry's ongoing IVF struggles, especially as their savings had been whittled down by ten thousand pounds in the process. They were like sisters; Carrie like the older one by two years.

She still felt warm and buzzed from the three gin and tonics she'd had with Nat at the bar, even after a quick stop at the newsagents on the corner of her street to pick up a box of luxury chocolates and a Valentine's Day card. Maybe the alcohol was a good thing; it gave her the confidence she needed to put her romantic plan into action. She unlocked the door to the communal hallway of her block of flats and took the lift up to the fourth floor, with a spring in her step.

Ken. They had met in the lift, a month ago, and she had found him attractive right away, with his olive skin, black hair and dark, warm eyes. What age was he? Late twenties, early thirties? Carrie couldn't say for sure; all she knew was that he was her type. What a disappointment to find out he had a girlfriend. She wasn't a homewrecker; she would never flirt with a man who was spoken for. She kept a polite, but friendly distance from him after his girlfriend started making regular visits to their apartment block. With its paper-thin walls, she could hear everything that went on between them. *Everything.* Their passionate sex, their arguments, what they watched on TV. The list went on.

But now he was free. Single and free, like her, on Valentine's Day.

She went inside her flat, switched on the lights and kicked off her shoes. Her mind was focused only on one task; to write the card, and then leave it – along with the chocolates – on his doorstep.

Carrie sat down on her bed and grabbed a pen, ready to write the card.

Dear Ken,

I would love to get to know you a bit more. Would you like to join me for a coffee sometime? Hope you enjoy these chocolates, just to say, Happy Valentine's Day.

Below the short note, she scribbled her number and looped a heart shape around it.

Bold, but Natalie was right. She needed to be decisive. She wrapped the chocolates in red crepe paper, taped the card on top of them, and took the stairs up one floor to leave her present outside Ken's flat.

***

What time was it? The gentle knocking on her door – three raps – had roused her from a light sleep. Carrie glanced at the time on her phone. Eleven thirty PM. Who could be at her door at such a late hour on Valentine's Day? She slid her feet into her fluffy slippers then padded out of her bedroom and along the hallway to answer the door.

Better to be cautious, especially in such a large block of flats. She peered through the peephole and saw Ken standing there, wearing black jeans and a red t-shirt, his hands in his pockets. He looked as handsome as ever as he waited in the corridor outside her flat.

Ken. Her heart practically exploded in her chest. She unclasped the safety chain and unlocked the bolt, then swung the door open, probably with too much vigour – but it was hard to contain her excitement.

"Er, hey. Carrie, isn't it?" Ken removed one hand from his pocket and smoothed his hair back, his cheeks crimson. The blush endeared him even more to me, if that was possible. I loved shy guys. Better than overconfident ones like Richard.

"Yeah, I'm Carrie." She twisted her fingers into good-luck signs behind her back.

"Just wanted to say, thanks for the chocolates." He suddenly looked bashful and hung his head. "Erm, and sorry for disturbing you so late in the evening."

"Oh, that's no bother at all. I was just–" She tucked her hair behind her ear, thinking quickly. "Watching TV."

Ken took a step back, giving her a shy smile. "Well, I'll leave you to that, then. But I have your number, right? I'll give you a call. Maybe we can grab that coffee?"

Her heart must have somersaulted, as she found herself unable to speak. All she could do was nod like a dashboard dog. Ken walked downstairs, a skip in his step, then shut the door. Overcome, Carrie danced on the spot and clapped her hands, squealing like an adolescent girl. Who cared? She deserved some romance on Valentine's Day, for once in her life. The only thing that could have made it better was if he had kissed her, right there on her doorstep. But the spark between them was good enough, for the time being.

Her feet felt lighter, like she was walking on the moon and her head was floating, light as a balloon as she padded back towards her bedroom. Light and laughter from her living room stopped her in her tracks. She opened the door and saw that the TV had sprung to life by itself. Weird. Must have been an electrical surge. Could electrical surges do that? She shrugged.

Come to think of it, watching something seemed like a good idea. She wouldn't be able to get herself back into a calm state to sleep right after something so exciting, like her hot neighbour turning up on her doorstep.

Settling down on the sofa, she found a good rom-com to watch. For once, she allowed herself to dissolve into a warm, fuzzy bliss and enjoy the remaining twenty-five minutes of Valentine's Day before the witching hour ended and she sank into a sleepy haze.

***

Carrie's phone buzzed in her pocket. Luckily she had remembered to put it on silent, or she would have had a bus full of angry commuters turning to glare at her. A notification from a number she didn't recognise popped up at the top of the screen. She had a gut feeling who it might be, and her heartbeat sped with anticipation as she unlocked my phone to read it.

Hey Carrie. Hope u don't have the Monday blues. How about a coffee later 2 cheer us both up? Ken :)

Normally she would have waited an hour or so to reply, but she couldn't help her excitement about Ken, and was happy to let him know. How long had it been since she'd met a guy who had given her such a strong connection? Call it Chemistry, whatever the explanation. She hadn't felt such *electricity* with anyone, ever before and the thought sent static waves coursing through her body.

That sounds lovely :) She texted back.

Great. Would the Coffee Lounge near r place work for u? Say 6?

How did he know that 6pm was the perfect time for her? It was usually the time she left her flat to meet friends after getting home and de-working herself into casual clothes.

6 is perfect. Looking fwd to it xx

Wonder what he would think of the two kisses at the end? Again, she didn't mind showing him how he made her feel. Wasn't it better to show passion right from the outset? Natalie was right; Carrie felt ready for a new romance. It most definitely was the best thing for her. Not all men were like Richard either. Ken was as different from her narcissistic ex as you could get.

Her day at work sailed by on a tide of bliss. She imagined herself with Ken. They would make a lovely couple; a tall, dark and handsome man in contrast with her petite red-headedness. She dared to imagine what their first kiss would be like; gentle and soft, or heavy and passionate. She dared to imagine more, but had to stop herself as she started getting funny looks in the office kitchen. Whew; those thoughts had to stay compartmentalised until later, when she could do something about them.

She felt like she was floating on the bus journey home, her mind on Ken. Eager for someone to share the excitement of her first date, she texted Natalie.

Hey Nat. U will never guess who I'm going to c 4 coffee.

Three little dots showed that she was typing back; probably at breakneck speed.

Who? Tell!

Carrie grinned at the screen.

Ken, she wrote back. She pictured Nat bringing her hands together in one single clap.

No way! Did u ask him out?

Carrie chortled to herself, imagining Nat's excitement on her behalf. *I gave him a card and chocolates like u said, Japanese-style. It worked.*

Omg that's so kewl!

Carrie's fingers tapped like wildfire. *Will let u know later xx*

She got off at her stop and turned right for the Coffee Lounge instead of left for their block of flats. Ken was already waiting outside. He wore a khaki-coloured jacket and black jeans. Her heart skipped a beat as his face broke into a wide grin when he saw her approaching.

"Hey Ken. Hope you weren't waiting long?" Carrie hesitated from leaning in for a hug, her natural instinct, teetering on the balls of her feet.

"Not at all. I just got here," he said, smiling. "How was your day?"

"It just got better," she said, offering a cheeky wink. Ken rewarded her with a gorgeous smile.

Wow, she had *certainly* struck lucky with such a good-looking man this time. Richard wasn't a patch on him.

"What about your day? Were you working?" she continued.

He shook his head, his smile fading a little. "I'm taking some time off work. Just going through some things."

Like a bad breakup. Carrie wanted to say it aloud, to tell him she could relate, to reassure him; but she didn't. What if he told her he still had feelings for his ex and wanted to get back together with her?

She shook the negative thoughts from her head. She needed to give their first date a chance. Maybe he would like spending time with her so much, he would forget his ex.

A couple came out as they went in; Ken hesitated as though he was going to hold the door for her, but she was too quick, going straight inside. Too much excitement. Damn. Would have been a chance for Ken to be her chivalrous knight-in-shining-armour. Oh well. Maybe the next time. Maybe they would have many future dates. Hopefully.

They approached the counter and looked at the menu.

"What'll it be?" said the barista.

"I'll have a skinny latte please," Carrie said.

"A black coffee for me, thanks," said Ken.

"Paying together, or separately?"

She glanced at Ken. "I'll get these. Technically I was the one who asked you out on a date, so it's my treat."

He gave a warm smile. "Alright then. Next time, I'll get them."

Next time. A tremor of excitement rippled through her; so he *did* like her more than she thought? She really felt like a teenager out with her first boyfriend, not a mature woman in her mid-thirties.

"I'll bring the drinks to your table," said the barista.

They took a seat at a cosy booth towards the back of the Coffee Lounge. The L-shaped seat allowed them to sit near each other, within touching distance if they wanted to, yet not mean they had to face each other directly. Hopefully that would prevent any awkward silences; they could chat, and people-watch too.

When their drinks arrived, she sipped in a comfortable silence, happy to enjoy Ken's company, but he looked down at his drink without touching it.

"I should be honest with you, Carrie. I've just come out of a rather messy relationship," he said, a note of sadness in his voice.

"How messy?" she said, a little too quick.

He let his eyes flit upwards to meet hers. "We were together for nine months. We had a messy breakup just last Friday."

"It's not–" she paused. "Too soon for our date, is it?"

He shook his head, but his face was grave. "It's the best thing that's happened to me in ages, honestly."

What did he mean by the best thing? Breaking up with his ex, or being on a date with her? She wanted to ask, but didn't want to come across as desperate.

"If it's any consolation, I recently broke up with someone too. My ex and I split up in November. I found out he was cheating on me." Carrie tried to keep her voice neutral, but there was a definite hint of bitterness that she couldn't keep from her words.

"Sorry to hear that," he said, his expression sad.

"Why did you break up with yours, if you don't mind me asking?" she went on.

"No, I don't mind. She wanted to move in with me, but I wasn't ready for that. I felt things were moving too fast. She was talking of marriage and kids. I wasn't sure I wanted either of those things." He glanced sideways at Carrie, before elaborating. "With her."

She smiled. "I'm sure you did the right thing for you."

"I know I did," he said, returning her smile.

What would Natalie think of all this? Carrie, counselling her new love interest, on their first date, about his clingy ex? She could imagine Nat telling her that she was right; it was too soon for a rebound thing.

Not if the sex was passionate though. She allowed the heat to sear in her cheeks at such a thought; whew.

Ken distracted her from her saucy thoughts as he stood up from their booth. "Please excuse me a moment."

She watched him walk towards the toilets, admiring his taut ass and muscular legs. It was only as he disappeared through the doors that she realised he hadn't touched his coffee. Guess they had been so wrapped up in their past love woes that he had forgotten about it.

Five minutes passed. She sipped her latte, her mind on what might happen once they left the café. She wasn't really a kiss-on-the-first-date kind of girl, never mind anything more, but if Ken made a move, she knew she wouldn't resist.

Ten minutes passed. Was Ken okay?

Fifteen minutes. She was starting to get worried. What if he'd had an accident in the toilets? Like, banged his head and passed out, that kind of thing. She finished her cold latte in two gulps, all too aware that he hadn't even touched his own coffee.

Twenty minutes. No, this was odd. Something was definitely wrong. She hadn't seen him coming out of the gents at all.

She approached the barista at the counter. "Erm, hello. The man I came in with hasn't come out of the toilets for about twenty minutes. I'm a bit worried he's alright. Would someone mind checking on him, please?"

The barista looked nonplussed, but without saying anything, he ventured into the gents. He returned a moment later.

"Nobody was in there," he said, before turning away from her. "Next, please."

What could she do? She exited the café, her chin hanging ever so slightly. Had Ken slipped out of the café unnoticed, while she had been lost in her thoughts? Somehow, she didn't think he had. Or was that simply wish fulfilment? Was she too desperate to meet a nice guy that she couldn't imagine the possibility that he might stand her up on a first date?

She truly felt depressed. She scuffed her shoes along the pavement as she walked back to her flat. Alone.

***

Several days passed. Three days, to be exact. What did it matter? The aftermath of that Monday following Valentine's Day on the weekend was a monotonous blur. Carrie cried copious tears into her pillow, snapped at her colleagues at work, and shoved past anyone on the bus during her commute, the weekday evenings trundling by in a lonely stampede.

Was Ken simply another heartless bastard in a long line of failed love affairs? Maybe she was destined to be sad and single and gathering dust on the shelf forever, long past her sell-by date. Natalie's eager texts following her disastrous date with Ken added yet more pain, even though she hadn't intended this at all.

Well, how was the big date?

She texted Nat back. *Not as I hoped.*

Oh? Good or bad?

Bad. He left halfway through. Just stood me up.

Work had got in the way of their consolation catch-up. Thursday evening came soon enough: tortillas, tears and yet another pep-talk from Nat about how she was too good for all the men she wound up on disastrous dates with.

Richard the cheating bastard.

Mr Psycho.

Mr Pervert.

And now Ken? Mr Ghost.

Yeah, it was a good nickname. He had ghosted her, for sure. She hadn't even received one single text from him since Monday. Not one. Despite texting him, just the once, to ask if he was okay. What a callous bastard.

After tortillas, of course, Nat got to go home to Barry. Always dinner or drinks with her on evenings when Barry had to work late. Carrie felt even more lonely as she trundled home to her flat – again – alone.

As she walked towards the lifts, the doors opened before she had a chance to hit the button. A woman walked out carrying a large sports bag, which must have been heavy, as it caused her to veer to the left to compensate for its bulk. She was so busy looking at the bag that it took her a moment to realise who the woman was.

Ken's ex.

Or current girlfriend?

As the woman passed her by, Carrie turned and looked over her shoulder, about to ask whether she was back with Ken again, before she came to her senses and stopped herself. Why bother? Ken had walked out on their first date before it had barely even started, and now his ex-girlfriend was leaving his flat carrying a big sports bag. They were clearly back together. The bag must have been an overnight holdall. She seemed the materialistic sort.

Carrie scoffed to herself as she got in the elevator. Bitch. And bastard. If he knew he was going to get back with his ex, he never should have agreed to their date.

And yet, he had seemed so sweet. So eager, as he had texted her. Eager as he had arrived on her doorstep, to thank her for the card and chocolates.

***

Rap, rap, rap. Three raps.

Carrie raised her chin off her chest and inhaled with a loud snort. She smacked her lips a couple of times and looked around, reorientating herself. She had fallen asleep on her sofa.

A pause, then another three raps. Who was that? Natalie? Maybe checking up on her? She highly doubted it would be Nat; she had given her friend no cause to worry about her over their tortilla meal.

Who then? She peered through the peephole and saw Ken. He was dressed casually in black jeans and a red t-shirt; pretty much the same clothes he had worn when he had arrived to woo her on Valentine's Day. Had to be an emotional ploy then. What did he want, a booty call? He could forget it.

She swung the door open, her jaw set.

"Carrie. It's good to see you," he said, his voice sad.

She blinked at him. Was he for real?

"What do you want?" she said, her voice as cold as she could muster.

He sighed. "I'm sorry I couldn't stay on Monday. It's difficult."

"It's difficult for me too," she said, cutting in quickly. "What happened?"

"I had to go." He held his palms out, defeated.

"Oh, so it's like *that*, is it? Well, I have to go *too*." She started to shut the door, but his hands, which had been hanging, were now raised in a pleading protest.

"Please. Give me a second chance. I didn't know what was going to happen."

"And I *did*? You think I like being stood up on a first date? You think that gives me a good impression of a guy?" She tossed her hair. "Listen, I have no time for games. Goodnight, Ken."

"Please. I'm begging you. Hear me out. Even for just one last chance. And then you can feel free to never see me again, if that's how it's meant to be."

The desperate, broken tone in his voice tugged on her heartstrings. Maybe she was being a fool. Maybe fate would prove her to be an idiot, with the fullness of time. But her romantic heart cried out to give him another chance – one last chance.

She opened the door.

Ken came in without a word, with only a soft, placid smile on his face. He kept his head low, his expression humble, his eyes on the carpet. That had to mean something, surely? Repentance? Remorse? He was no narcissist; she knew that much. She got the sense he wasn't cheating on her either; he was finished with his ex, for good.

Carrie closed the door behind him and placed the safety chain on the lock; a habitual, big city action on her part. He led the way through to her living room. She had been watching a baking show on Netflix before she fell asleep; as they entered the living room, the TV suddenly malfunctioned, black wiggly lines sizzling across the screen accompanied by the hissing of static.

"Sorry, it's temperamental these days. Let me switch it off," she apologised.

As if on cue, the TV blacked out entirely.

Ken sat down on one end of the grey sofa, and she perched awkwardly on the other end. Did she sense an excuse coming on? One could only hope.

"I really owe you an explanation," Ken started.

Carrie said nothing, watching him, her head leaning on one hand, her elbow propped up against the sofa.

"Chantelle came to get her stuff earlier," he went on.

"So I saw," she added, her voice gruff.

He rubbed his throat, as if finding the right words was difficult. "We're done for good. I thought you should know that. It's important to me that you know I'm not that kind of guy. You know, the sort who plays two women off against each other."

"A cheater?" she prompted, her voice full of coldness.

Ken swallowed, his Adam's apple bobbing with the gulp. "Right, a cheater. I've never cheated, and never would. But things are complicated."

"Like, you mean, you need more time?"

His wide, brown eyes fixed on her then. There was an innocent intensity to his expression that struck her; froze her to the spot. Took the air right out of her chest.

"Time? There's never enough. Time escapes me. I have so much to do, and so little time to do it in." He took a breath. "I met you at the wrong time."

Once again, his gaze made her freeze. She felt as though a spotlight was focused on her, rendering her immobile. All she could do was stare at him.

"I think I get it. You mean to say, you like me, but the timing isn't right?" she said, her tone softening.

He shook his head, his face drawn and sad. "I like you, but I wish we had met at a better *time*."

Carrie digested his words. She was tempted to argue that he had said precisely the same thing as she had, only in a more pretentious way; but she decided against. He was suffering as much as she was. Richard – and Chantelle – could go to hell. All that mattered was how things would progress between her and Ken.

He dared a glance at her. "I feel very strongly for you. There's an intense connection. I felt it from the moment I knocked on your door."

What about the time they had met in the lift, when he had still been with his ex-girlfriend? She wanted to ask but didn't dare.

He seemed to have read her mind. "I found you attractive from the moment I saw you in the lift, a few months back, but I was still with Chantelle then."

She nodded her understanding, but said nothing.

"I told you on our date that she wanted to move in with me, and that we'd had a big fight about it," he went on.

A fight she had heard from the screams and thuds above; but didn't say. She nodded for him to continue.

"She came to my flat drunk and threatened to kill herself if I left her. She said she would throw herself out of my bedroom window. She even grabbed my favourite teddy bear – an antique that my nan had given me when I was a toddler – and said she would do it right then."

Carrie shook her head. "That's awful. What did you do?"

"I managed to snatch the bear away from her, but knocked the lamp over in the process. I'm sorry for the commotion. You must have heard the crash."

"It's no bother, these things happen." She couldn't say why, but she needed to hear more of his story.

"I realised she was a manipulative, dangerous narcissist at that point, and that I had to rid myself of her. So I ushered her out of my flat – and out of my life. But you have to understand that nine months of an intense whirlwind – however toxic – has an impact on a person," he said.

She could definitely relate. An image of Richard's smug face flitted into her mind.

"I didn't have an easy upbringing. My mother turned alcoholic after my granny died. She worked a day shift in a supermarket and did more shady things at night to fund her habit. My younger brother and I were terrified of the men who came in and out of our flat. When I was twelve, I was big enough to square up to a few of them if it seemed like they might get handy with my mum. Social services took us away when Mikey's primary school got involved and we were put into care."

"Oh Jeez, I'm so sorry to hear all this," Carrie said, unsure of how to console him.

"It's okay, you don't have to be, it's in the past. Besides, my social worker helped me to get my own flat when I turned sixteen and when I was eighteen, I became a temporary carer for Mikey, who was fifteen then, until he became an adult legally too. That's when I moved here for work, and I've been here for six years."

"And then you met Chantelle?" Carrie asked, unable to keep the sadness from her voice.

"Not right away. I had a few other less serious relationships that fizzled out. We just didn't click. Chantelle was intense and passionate – things that I liked about her at first. But she was also a verbally abusive drunk." Ken held up his hand. "I'll stop, I don't want to turn you into my therapist. The point is, I needed to sort out my chaotic life and a string of dysfunctional relationships – and that included my relationship with myself."

They both sat in silence, ruminating. She could relate. How many broken relationships with users who disrespected her had she been through? Too many to count.

"At least you and I took a chance with each other, and on Valentine's Day," she said, her voice an octave higher, full of hope.

He smiled; the first she'd seen since he'd arrived. A good sign.

"I've made a mess of my life. I think I've gone too far this time, you know, like beyond the point of no return." His voice was cracked, but he raised his eyes then to meet hers. "But I've enjoyed spending time with you and getting to know you. It helps me to forget the aftermath of the mess I made."

"You didn't make a mess." Carrie waved her hand to dismiss his fears. "And you aren't beyond hope. It's a fresh start for you, just like it's a fresh start for me as well. I enjoy spending time with you too."

She reached for his hand, and felt a sting of static electricity jump between her index finger and his pinky finger. Despite her automatic recoil from the sting, she took the static as another good sign. They were both clearly so charged with positive emotions that they created an electrical sting when they touched.

Carrie slipped her hand inside his. His fingers were cold, with a slight clamminess as though he was coming down with a fever. Of course, he was only wearing a t-shirt, so maybe he *had* caught a chill; and relaying the sadness of his past couldn't have helped. A comfortable calm came over her, to the point where she began to feel sleepy once more. She hoped that some of the happy energy that had surged through her transferred across to Ken through their touch. He deserved to be happy too.

***

A stream of sunlight cut a thick wedge across the living room, flooding in through a gap in the curtain. Carrie focused on the dust particles dancing in the light for a few moments, allowing herself to wake.

Had she slept on the sofa? What on earth? She hadn't been drunk the previous evening; she had gone for tortillas with Nat and had enjoyed a few margaritas, but she hadn't even been tipsy, never mind drunk.

She looked down at herself; she was still wearing yesterday's clothes. She swiped her fingers across her eyelashes and felt the crustiness of her mascara.

What was going on? She always made sure to take off her makeup, get into her pyjamas and get herself into bed. Falling asleep fully clothed on the sofa with last night's makeup still on was a first.

Where was Ken? The previous evening rushed back into her mind. At some point during the night, while she had been dozing on the sofa, Ken had rapped on the door. She recalled with clarity everything he had told her about his relationship with Chantelle, and his damaged home life. They had held hands on the sofa. Had she dozed off again?

Ken must have slipped out quietly while she slept. It unnerved her that the door must surely have been unlocked. Their apartment block was relatively secure; but she always made sure to have the bolt locked and the safety chain on anyway. Such was big city life.

Carrie padded down the hallway in her slippers to check.

The door was locked, and safety chain still on.

Odd. That meant Ken had to be still inside her flat, didn't it?

She walked through to her bedroom. The bed was still made, as she had left it before work the previous morning, the duvet smooth without even one crease.

There wasn't a chance Ken had chosen to sleep on her bedroom floor where the double bed would block view of him? She wandered towards the window so that she could see the floor on the other side of her bed.

No, not there either.

"Ken?" Carrie called. "Hey Ken, are you in here?"

She knocked on the bathroom door before turning the handle. Not in there.

Checked the kitchen; empty.

Checked the hallway storage cupboard just for completeness; not there either.

Her curiosity turned to bewilderment, which festered into an unsettling blankness. An information gap. She couldn't, through any rational explanation, think of where Ken had gone.

There were only two options; and neither of them seemed likely.

Option number one was that she had dreamed of the whole conversation with Ken in her flat. Was that likely? What if her love-starved brain had concocted the whole apology-explanation-romantic connection as a way of giving her reconciliation with Ken standing her up in the Coffee Lounge and then ghosting her for days afterwards? Was that something her brain was likely to do? Not really. Then again, neither was falling asleep fully clothed on her sofa. She gave it a likelihood ranking of 6 out of 10, with 10 being completely likely.

Option number two sent a chill down her spine. What if Ken really had come to her flat, and they really had talked about his past and held hands on the sofa. He confided that Chantelle had threatened to throw herself out of his bedroom window. What if he had done the same thing by throwing himself out of *her* bedroom window. After all, the conversation – on his part – had ended on a melancholy note.

Carrie walked once more into her bedroom, her shoulders stiffened to brace herself as she prepared to look out the bedroom window. What might she see? His crumpled body on the pavement below, a pool of blood around him? Surely if that were the case, she would hear commotion on the street below, and the wail of sirens would have roused her from my slumber in the living room.

She took a deep, calming breath and opened the window. The street below was normal, with commuters passing to and fro and traffic as normal. No telltale pool of blood, or yellow and black police cordon signs. She gave option number two a ranking of 1 out of 10; highly unlikely.

With her head hanging, Carrie slouched through into the kitchen. She must have dreamed of the whole scenario with Ken. Her brain was a callous, cruel tormentor to fabricate such a dream that had backfired by making her feel even more lonely and sad than ever. She poured a bowl of muesli and scrolled through her text messages, stopping at Ken's name.

What if she texted him? It couldn't hurt, could it? It was her one chance of proper closure on their non-existent relationship, wasn't it? She couldn't hurt herself any more than how she already felt; so she had nothing to lose.

Hey Ken she texted, then paused, formulating her words. *I really enjoyed catching up over coffee on Monday. Would u like to go for dinner some time? Xx*

Send. Now all she had to do was wait. Hopefully he wouldn't keep ghosting her and at least would let her know what was up.

Three little dots appeared below her text, and her heart skipped a beat. He was writing back. She held her breath as she watched the wiggling dots.

I enjoyed coffee, and I liked last nite 2. Thanks for being so understanding. :)

Carrie released her breath and gulped. *I liked last nite 2.*

Then it *had* happened. She hadn't dreamed anything. Ken had been in her flat, and they had chatted, in the early hours. Three more little dots appeared.

Dinner sounds great. XX

She swallowed a spoonful of cornflakes, staring at her phone. She had to know the mystery of the chain on her front door.

I loved talking last night too. I fell asleep on the sofa, guess I was so relaxed. What time did u leave?

Three little dots. His reply pinged on her phone.

I don't remember. I think I dozed at one point on ur sofa 2. Must've been so relaxed myself. Woke up in my bed.

Weird. Could both of them have been so sleepy that she had seen Ken out of her flat, and then locked the door behind him? If so, had they exchanged a goodnight kiss? Her brain was relegated back to the category of cruel if it had given her a sleep-induced-memory-blank during any a much longed-for goodnight kiss.

Not that such a thing mattered right now. All that mattered was that Ken hadn't ghosted her and they were reconciled. Both of them were free of their exes; whatever happened next was up to the stars.

***

Destiny. Fate. Desire. Romance.

For once, all these things were on her side. Carrie's heart was an open book, ready for a new chapter. Ready for the kind of love that she finally deserved.

Her chest swelled with a deep, healing, inhale.

She wasn't the best cook, but she wanted dinner to be special. Perfect. Being single, she tended to make herself simple meals like Spaghetti Bolognese or chicken with sweet and sour from a jar. This time, she had made steak in a peppercorn sauce with garlic potatoes and tender-stem broccoli.

Just in time; three raps on the door announced that Ken had arrived. She took off her apron, turned the heat off the cooker and fixed her hair over her shoulders as she went to answer the door. Hopefully her hair cascaded in tumbling waves that didn't smell of garlic potatoes.

Ken's mouth dropped as she opened the door, and his eyes travelled down, then back up her body.

"Carrie, you look amazing."

He held a posey of red roses in one hand and reached for a hug with the other. A swirl of cold air breezed around them both, giving her a slight shiver; her satin dress that cut in under the bust and billowed to the tops of her thighs was perfect for a warm flat, but not the draughty communal hallways of their apartment building.

"Come in," she ushered. "Dinner is ready."

Ken stepped inside and she locked the door behind him, setting the safety chain back on the lock. He handed her the posey of roses, with a grin over the top of them.

"A belated Valentine's Day present for a beautiful woman," he said.

Carrie felt heat sizzle in her cheeks as she spun for him. Her satin dress was red with white polka dots; the sexiest dress she had that still didn't try too hard. It had an element of cuteness, and the flared style allowed for a stomach full of steak and potatoes; a perfect dinner-dress.

She led him through to the kitchen and watched a wide smile slowly spread across his face as he saw the food on the cooker. "I can't believe you made all this for me. This looks fantastic."

After gesturing to him to sit, she checked that the steak was cooked right by cutting a small slice through to the middle of the larger one. She served the larger of the two steaks for Ken, as it was also the nicer looking of the pair, along with a scoop of garlic potatoes and broccoli. Then she opened a bottle of Pinot Noir, her favourite, and poured two large glasses.

Ken leaned over his plate and inhaled. "This smells incredible. I can't wait to try a bite."

"Happy belated Valentine's Day." They clinked glasses. "Tuck in."

The meal was scrumptious, even if she said so herself. Amazing how she was able to rustle up food that was cooked just right. Multitasking on the cooker usually ended with her burning the sauce and under-cooking the rice or pasta. Either that or something boiling over and making a huge, bubbling mess. This time, everything was *perfect*.

They ate in silence, savouring the food for the first few minutes. Watching Ken's contented face as he ate gave Carrie great pleasure. The old saying about the way to a man's heart being through his belly jumped to mind. She sure hoped so. She had high hopes for what might happen after they'd eaten and polished off the wine.

"Where did you learn to cook?" said Ken.

"A few recipe books and cooking shows, and maybe one or two Instagram accounts. But other than that, I guess I like experimenting with food," she said.

"Well, it certainly shows. You're an amazing cook, Carrie."

She grinned. Feeling bold, she decided to test the waters for later. "A cook in the kitchen and in the bedroom – ahem. You know how the saying goes."

Ken's face crinkled as he laughed, showing two rows of even, white teeth. God, he was gorgeous. And – thank God – he had taken her joke well.

"We'll see about that," he chortled, letting his laughter subside. An amorous look replaced it. Her body tingled at suddenly becoming the object of such a sexy man's desire.

Ken stood up and she rose with him, taking the cue. His hands swept towards her face, cupping her cheeks as he lowered his face to hers for an intense, and passionate kiss. She noted that his hands still felt cold, despite how hot it was in her kitchen. Not to worry; the electrical tingles that sizzled through her at his touch made up for that.

Time for the dessert course. She broke away from Ken's kiss to lead him to her bedroom, the tips of their fingers intwined as she tugged, and he followed. As they kissed again, his hands reached behind her and unzipped her dress. She felt him reach for the clasp of her bra and unhook it first go. Impressive. It only made her desire him more.

Sex with Ken was every bit as amazing as she had imagined it would be; maybe even more passionate. His touch – hands and mouth – on her body sent cold, electrical tingles all over. She found the sensation to be unlike anything she had felt before; and also intensely erotic. His lips on her neck, breasts, stomach – and other areas, carried a cold sting, as though he had been eating a menthol sweet before putting his mouth on her skin. There was no warm, wet, heavy pressure when their bodies joined as had been her experience of intercourse every time since she had first lost her virginity at sixteen; instead, their lovemaking felt incredibly light, as cool, sizzling static stimulated her body inside and out. Carrie found herself able to climax much quicker, and with a deeper, more intense orgasm than she had ever experienced before. The sensation brought her to tears as her pent-up emotions poured out, her libido a lava flow of release. Ken finished at the same time as her and lay on top of her body, a lightweight and cool blanket enveloping her. Unable to stop herself, her breathing steadied and slowed, and her eyes closed.

***

Her bladder full of red wine roused Carrie in the darkness and she blinked her eyes open, staring at her bedroom ceiling for a few moments to let herself fully wake.

She was still naked, the duvet pulled up over her breasts and her arms above the cover.

What a magical evening. She rolled her head to the side and saw that Ken was sleeping peacefully on his side, facing away from her.

She kissed his ear, lightly so as not to wake him, then slid out her side of the bed and walked to the bedroom door. As she opened it, a flood of light from the hallway streamed in. Carrie pulled the door shut behind her, so that the brightness wouldn't wake Ken, then went to the bathroom to wee.

While she relieved her bladder, she smiled to herself. If their first sex session was anything to go by, then her love life was suddenly going to be propelled to stratospheric levels. She let her grin widen at the thought. Best sex she'd ever had in her life.

Carrie walked back to her bedroom, feeling in seventh heaven, and opened the door. The hallway light flooded in once more. She was about to step in and quickly pull the door shut behind, when the wedge of light falling across the bed made her stop in her tracks.

Her side of the bed was empty, where she had thrown the duvet cover back to go take a wee. On Ken's side the duvet was piled up in a bulge that looked child-sized at best; but not big enough to cover a tall man.

She made no move to shut out the hallway light as she approached Ken's side of the bed and touched the bulge. It felt soft. She pressed harder with her hand, and it flattened. Confused, she pulled back the cover.

Empty.

Empty bed, and empty chill. Yes, a cold, empty sickness began to well in the pit of her stomach. What was going on? She had seen Ken asleep in her bed moments before and had heard his soft breathing as he slept. No way she had imagined things, nor had she been dreaming; and she certainly wasn't crazy.

What was going on? Carrie felt sick. Steak, and wine, pooled in her stomach as she pondered the empty bed.

She clapped both hands against her forehead and stared at the inexplicable sight of her empty double bed.

She switched on the bedroom light and grabbed her fluffy dressing gown from the back of the bedroom door. Tying the rope around her waist, she walked to the front door to investigate.

The chain was on the catch.

Bile rose in her throat. She slapped a hand over her mouth, turned and ran to vomit in the toilet.

***

"What do you make of all this?" Carrie said.

Natalie stared at her and circled the rim of her coffee mug with her index finger.

"It's nuts, that's what I think. It's seriously messed up. It's the weirdest thing I've ever heard," she said.

"But what do you think is going on? How can Ken just be there one moment, and not the next? Is he sneaking out somehow, in a way I don't know about, and messing with me?"

Nat blinked at her, across her kitchen table. "Why would he do that though?"

"Yeah, I guess he wouldn't. I mean, he seems so honest, like, legitimately a nice guy. He really seems to care about me. And the sex – oh *boy*. The sex was out of this world."

Nat gave her a cheeky knowing grin.

"The funny thing is, whatever is going on with him, I'm intoxicated. I'm in too deep now to back out. I'm more weirded out by him disappearing the morning after, rather than angry, if you get what I mean."

"Kind of." Nat narrowed her eyes. "That's infatuation talking, not logic."

Carrie let her chin slump into her hand. "Yeah, I guess so."

Silence fell between them for a moment. "Well, whatever is going on, I just hope he answers my texts. Two days have passed, and I've heard nothing," she said.

Nat's eyebrows dipped inwards. "Hopefully he isn't a creep. I mean, I really hope he isn't just showing up to use you as a booty call, and then disappearing."

Such a thought hadn't occurred to her. Could Ken be using her, like all the rest of her exes? He seemed so sweet, kind and caring; but could it all be a front? A means to an end to manipulate and seduce her?

Whatever look she had on her face seemed to have roused some sympathy – or pity – in Nat, for she turned her lip downwards, giving her a cute pout. "I'm sure he isn't though, Carrie. You're an amazing woman and I'm sure he knows that too."

"Well, whatever the reason for his full-on passion followed by disappearing acts, I'm used to it by now. I have a long history of being stood up." Carrie wanted to cry but didn't.

Nat squeezed her hand. "Did you send him a follow-up text?"

She nodded. "Three of them. I gave up after that."

She pushed her phone under Nat's nose and watched her eyes skim left to right over the texts:

Hey Ken, missed you leaving this morning. Everything OK?

Then, six hours later:

Is anything up? xx

Still no response, so the following day:

Not sure what happened, but I'll leave it up to you to get in touch, if you like. Bye - C xx

The texts only made their night of pleasure burn all the more, charring a larger slice of her heart than the last time.

"Well, more fool him if he wants to lose an amazing, and beautiful woman like you," said Nat, giving her hand a reassuring stroke.

Carrie shook her head. "It doesn't add up though – that's not all. When we were having dinner, I watched him eating the steak and veg that I cooked, as well as drink the wine. But when I checked the kitchen after I realised he was gone, you'll never believe the strangest thing."

Nat stared at me, unblinking, hanging onto my every word.

"The steak hadn't been touched, all except for the single cut that I had made to the middle of it, to check that it was well cooked. Nothing else looked touched either – the broccoli, potatoes, or wine."

Her best friend's eyes were wide and haunted. "That doesn't make any sense, though."

"I know, that's what I thought too. I mean, there's no way I could have imagined the whole thing, could I?"

Nat raised both eyebrows. "You're not crazy, if that's what you mean. You're the most sane person I know. In fact, so sane, that I'd say you're even on the *stiff* side."

Carrie grinned. Nat was right though. She tended to be a logical, rational person. Definitely not someone who was prone to an overactive imagination; to an extent that it would cause her to gaslight herself.

No, there had to be a rational explanation. She looked around her kitchen. Nat was sitting in the seat where Ken had sat. Before they sat down to eat, he had given her flowers.

"Oh Jeez, Nat. You know what? Ken gave me a bunch of roses that night, when I invited him here for dinner."

"Where did you put them?" she said, looking around too.

Carrie thought hard, recalling the sequence of events from after Ken stepped inside her flat.

"He gave them to me in the hallway, and I came in here holding them, but got distracted by the food on the cooker." She let her eyes slide sideways along the counter. There, sticking out from behind the bread bin, was the posey.

Both of them jumped up at once. Carrie grabbed the flowers by their stems, still wrapped in paper. The red roses had wilted somewhat, their petals turning brown.

"I *didn't* imagine the whole thing. I'm not crazy," she gasped.

"Maybe just a little," Nat joked. "But only a touch."

She smiled, but the guilt kept her from laughing. "Do you think that's why Ken stood me up? Do you think I hurt him because I didn't put these in a vase of water?"

Nat shrugged. "Doubt it. He wouldn't have fucked your brains out if he'd been so offended."

Fair point.

Nat bent to sniff the flowers. She recoiled with her tongue protruding, her upper lip curled. "Ugh. What's with those flowers? They stink like rotten meat."

Carrie bent to take a whiff too, then winced. Nat was right. Why hadn't she noticed before? The stench was overpowering.

"Flowers don't smell like that," she said, confused.

"You must have spilled some blood from the steak on them." Nat grabbed the bunch and dropped them in the pedal bin.

"I suppose. Though, the steak was pretty well-cooked by that point. And that's besides the fact they were nowhere near the food."

She dashed to open all the windows and let fresh air cleanse the flat.

"The mystery of Ken continues," Nat laughed. Carrie couldn't agree more.

***

"Pippa's a really easy cat. She won't be any bother for you. Apart from eating, she likes to sleep, so she'll make great company – a furry cushion for your sofa, really," Nat explained, as she stood in Carrie's hallway, holding the cat carrying box.

Carrie ducked to look at the contented ginger cat nestling in the box. "I'm amazed at how chill she is, especially since she's never been to my flat before."

Nat beamed. "I think you girls will have such fun. You'll be wanting a cat of your own at the end of the weekend."

"You could just let me adopt her now and save yourself the bother," she joked.

Nat set the carrier down and threw her arms around her. "Thanks so much, really, Barry and I owe you a big one for this."

"It's no bother at all. We'll probably cuddle up on the sofa and watch a romcom, and cry."

Nat raised an eyebrow. "What, still no appearance from Mister Valentino then?"

Mister Valentino was her new nickname for Ken, after their night of passion four days before. It was a suitable nickname in all honesty, as their romance had first kindled on Valentine's Day night, which was now four weeks' ago. Would Ken ever get back in touch? Carrie allowed herself a momentary visualisation of them as a happy couple, next Valentine's Day, celebrating the one-year anniversary of their meet-cute. The fleeting thought was replaced by sadness. She had yet to receive even a perfunctory follow-up text from him. Guess their passionate dinner-date night meant nothing, then.

"No. I'm tired of the guessing games to be honest. Seems like it was yet another ill-fated romance."

"He doesn't know what he's missing," said Nat, swooping in to kiss her cheek. "How about we hit the town when I'm back and see if we can find a date who's more deserving of you?"

"I could definitely do with that," she answered, hugging Nat.

Carrie waved Nat off and shut the door, then opened the cat carrier box to let Pippa out. She sat hunched in the box, both front paws tucked together.

"Hey Pippa, you want to come out for a snack? I've got one of your favourite treats."

The cat didn't move. Her eyes were like saucers at a point behind Carrie. Nat had predicted that Pippa might feel strange in her flat, which was why she had suggested using her favourite treats to entice her out of the carrier box.

She crouched down and reached into the box, but the cat moved further back until her rump was touching the back of the box. Pippa's round, fearful eyes were glued further along the hallway behind her.

Instinct made her turn. As she looked over her left shoulder, for a fraction of a second, she could have sworn she saw Ken standing in the shadow at the end of the hall. With a gasp, she jumped to her feet and swivelled to survey the spot where his image had been.

Was she going mad?

Whew, she had to get Ken off her mind. Obsessing about a date who clearly didn't feel nearly as strongly for her as she did for him was warping her mind. She turned her attention back to Pippa, scooped her out of the carrier, and headed for the living room.

What to watch? Maybe not a romcom; a true crime show was a better choice to get her thoughts off anything amorous.

Carrie switched on the box and settled with Pippa on her knee. The cat seemed content, nestling on her lap. She stroked her with an idle hand while browsing with the other for something good to watch.

Halfway through a show about serial killers, she began to get a strange feeling; like eyes watching her from behind. Even the tiny hairs on the back of her neck seemed electrified. Pippa began to make a strange, anguished cry; a shrill noise that sounded more like a tormented newborn than a cat. Carrie twitched her head to one side, looking out of the corner of her eye, and saw a tall shadow in the corner of the living room through her peripheral vision. She spun around.

Nobody. Nothing was there.

She wasn't imagining things. The atmosphere was charged, as though a person had been standing there a moment before.

What was going on? Seemed she was wrong about choosing a true crime show to watch; such a topic was making her jumpy.

"Let's get some lights on, shall we?" Pippa slid off her lap and onto the cushion, letting her stand up to turn on the lights. No point allowing shadows to pool and cause her imagination to go into overdrive.

Lights were the best things to chase away fears. Carrie walked through every room in her flat and switched on all the lights, electricity bill be damned.

Comfort food; that would be the next thing to calm her overactive mind. She grabbed a pizza from the freezer, tore it out of the plastic wrapper and stuck it in the oven.

As she turned away from the oven to get herself a plate from the cupboard, she nearly tripped over Pippa, who had followed her into the kitchen.

Were cats clingy? She had always thought of them as independent; at least, what little she knew about them, at any rate. The little ginger cat stalked behind her as she made a triangle from cupboard, to counter and back to the oven, making her strange and mournful cry. She closed the distance between them and placed herself between Carrie's legs where she cowered.

"What's going on Pip?" she said, reaching to stroke the tiny, fearful ginger ball.

As had happened in the hallway when she first peered out of her carrier box, Pippa's eyes were large, round saucers as they focused on a point towards the kitchen sink.

She bent to look at Pippa, then looked across to the kitchen sink, then back to Pippa.

"Carrie," said a man's voice behind her.

Carrie screamed and clapped a hand against her chest. Had she really heard her name being called? The voice was male. Not just male; it sounded exactly like Ken's.

From the living room, the crime show she had been watching droned on and she heard the words: *carry on with the inspection.*

Her heartbeat slowed. Maybe she was mistaken. Maybe she hadn't heard her name but had heard the actor on TV in the crime show saying 'carry on'.

Why was she being so jumpy and irrational?

And yet.

Yet.

There was definitely an energy in the kitchen, like there had been in the living room; the feeling of another person's presence. A whiff of cologne drifted under her nose. This time she knew she hadn't made any mistake; it was Ken's aftershave.

The fresh, masculine fragrance faded and a second later, a rotten stench caught in the back of Carrie's nostrils, almost making me gag. The smell reminded her of the wilted roses Ken had gifted her, though she had taken those out to the communal dumpster days before. As the horrible smell began to dissipate, she noticed a shadow drift across the cupboards and fade into the wall; almost like a shadow created by a cloud moving across the sun.

An involuntary shiver rippled through her, and with it, an electrical surge. Once the cold, static feeling disappeared, the kitchen felt normal and warm as usual.

Weird. No more crime shows; it would only be comedy films for the rest of the weekend. She got her pizza out of the oven, sliced it on the plate, and led Pippa into the living room.

Knock knock. Two raps at the door alerted her to a visitor. Could it be Ken? Ken usually knocked three times. If it wasn't him, then who could it be?

She hurried to unlock the door and swung it open. A small white box, with a red ribbon tied in a bow on top, lay on her doorstep. She lifted it and flipped open the attached gift tag.

To Carrie. Happy White Day.

White Day? What was that?

Wait a moment; the conversation with Nat on Valentine's Day, when she said that on February 14th, Japanese women gave chocolates to men as a proposal, then waited for an acceptance, or a rejection on March 14th.

White chocolates for yes, and cookies for no, on White Day.

Carrie unwrapped the box in her hands. Inside were twelve beautiful, artisanal white chocolates. One, designed like a snail shell, had raspberry threaded throughout. Another looked to be a nut-cluster. She selected one that looked to have honeycomb chunks embedded and bit into it.

Divine. Tears poured down her face. Ken had given her an answer. He had said 'yes' to her chocolate proposal on Valentine's Day, and in the same manner of her gift; by leaving it on her doorstep.

Why, then, the elusiveness after their dinner date in her flat followed by their night of passion?

Her phone buzzed in her pocket. She tapped to check the notification and saw a text from Ken.

Hey Carrie. Hope u like my answer?

Her heart soared as she tapped a response. *Yes, love it. Where are you?*

Three little dots, then: *I'm waiting in the foyer. Want 2 show u something.*

Mysterious. Her brain raced, trying to think. *I'm intrigued.*

His response. *Bring a coat.*

She paused. A coat? Where did he want to take her? A dinner date? Coffee? Her mind danced in a dizzying whirl of bliss.

The rational side of her took over. What should she wear? She was in her lounge clothes; an old t-shirt and tracksuit trousers. Also, what about Pippa? She couldn't leave the cat unattended in a strange place, and she had promised Nat she was free for cat-sitting.

What should I wear? Also, how long will it take? I'm cat-sitting she texted back. Regret spliced her mind; what if he thought she was no longer keen, or had better things to do than come with him on a secret expedition? It was so hard to put all her rogue thoughts into a text.

Ken responded: *Wear what ur in, u look beautiful always. Just need a coat. Bring the cat and some money for the train.*

Train money? If she was going anywhere further than their block of flats, she wasn't going to be seen in her lounge clothes.

Give me five mins. Just want to get ready.

Carrie dashed into her bedroom and flung on a pair of tight-fitting jeans and a blouse that accentuated her bust. With Pippa in her carrier, she then got her shoes and coat on and grabbed her phone and handbag.

Ken was waiting in the foyer. He wore a navy suit in a style suitable for a job interview, or a wedding, rather than a casual encounter.

"Ken, Jeez. Why didn't you tell me this was a formal thing? I'm in jeans."

Ken gave an apologetic grin, his head bowed. "Sorry," he said. "But I meant what I said, you look lovely in anything you wear."

"That isn't the point." She gave a teasing grin. "But, you *are* cute, so, I forgive you."

They kissed. The familiar cool sting of his lips as they met hers sent a shockwave of ecstasy through her body.

"I'm glad you like my present." His smile diminished, just a little. "There's something I need to show you though, something very important."

What could it be? Holding the handle of Pippa's carrier with a tight grip, she followed Ken out of their apartment building.

They walked in silence towards the train station. It was a comfortable silence. She loved they could be that way, and so soon into their relationship. There weren't many people she could be around and feel so at ease with, without having the need to fill every pause in conversation with empty chatter. They enjoyed the sensation of each other, as they walked side by side with Pippa in the middle. The little ginger cat *sure* was difficult to carry, considering she was so lightweight. A haunting, fearful cry emanated from the carrier, and the box swung from side to side as she did somersaults inside it.

She broke the comfortable silence. "Oh, be calm, you silly girl. What's bothering you?"

"Maybe she doesn't like me." Ken's mournful tone was only half-joking.

She winked at him. "That's nonsense. Who wouldn't like you?"

They entered the train station and she topped up her travel card. As she turned to cross the ticket barrier, she saw that Ken was already waiting on the other side, hands in his pockets and a placid smile on his face.

The train journey was short, and they spent it – once more – in a comfortable silence. Ken looked down at his hands, which he had placed with fingertips touching. The noise of the motion and distraction of commuters talking was enough distraction for Pippa, who settled in her carrier box on the train floor.

"This is our stop." Ken got off the train first, and Carrie followed him out of the station, into the growing twilight.

"I can't wait to see what it is that you want to show me," she said.

Ken looked away, but not before she had seen a glimmer of sadness in his eyes. What on earth?

They walked along a quiet, suburban street towards an old church. Was he taking her to meet his family? Her enquiring mind couldn't think of any other reason why they would be in such a sleepy neighbourhood full of semi-detached houses.

Of course, Ken had said that he had left his broken home many years before, as his alcoholic mother hadn't been able to take care of him and his younger brother.

To her surprise, Ken led her through the open iron gate into the churchyard. They weren't going to attend a service, were they?

"Are we eloping then?" she joked. "You aren't bringing me here to marry me on White Day, are you?"

"Sadly nothing that romantic," came his cryptic response.

Intriguing. As they drew closer, she noticed that the lights weren't on in the old church. Ken walked towards the front doors, then veered right and trod a path around to the back of the church, where she saw a graveyard, bathed in the light of the full moon.

She stopped in her tracks, as Pippa let out a long, low, frightened cry.

"What are we doing here?" The suspicion in her words was heavy, in the still air of the graveyard.

He answered in a neutral tone. "Bear with me, just a bit longer. The thing I need to show you is close by."

They walked in single file. She couldn't help but notice that the moonlight cast a pearly glow around Ken. As the evening progressed, the lamp-post light from the nearby residential street added more brightness to his outline, until it almost seemed he was ethereal.

She had been so distracted by her thoughts that when Ken stopped, she almost tripped over one of the gravestones.

"We're here." He gestured to the headstone.

Carrie looked at the headstone, then back at Ken, confused.

"This is what I wanted you to see," he continued.

She looked again at the headstone, and this time she read the name.

Kenneth Alan Rutherford.

"Who is this?" she asked.

Ken turned from the gravestone with a regretful expression.

She blinked at him. "Are you saying that this is your grave?"

He bit his lip and lowered his head.

Carrie couldn't help laughing. "Is this a joke?"

Ken shook his head. "I'm afraid it's real."

She took a step back, processing his words in combination with his serious expression. It didn't seem like he was kidding around. "I don't understand. You're standing there. Are you saying that you bought a burial plot? But why? You're young. You have so much to live for."

A pained expression creased his face, and the realisation sank in; he was being completely honest with her.

He stooped and tapped the date on the headstone. "I didn't buy a plot. My body is in that grave."

She forced her gaze to land on the engraved date his finger touched. The date of death was Valentine's Day.

Nausea rose in her gullet. Staggering back a few steps, she leaned against a nearby tree for support.

"I don't understand. How? Are you saying you're a ghost?" She dismissed his words with a wave. "No, there's a mistake. You can't be dead."

"It took me a while to get my head round it too," he said, with a sigh.

"No. This isn't possible. Ghosts don't exist." Her voice wavered, the fear in it palpable in her own ears.

"I used to think so too, until this happened to me."

"*What* happened to you? *What* exactly?"

He sat down on the grave, cross-legged. "We met at a bad time," he started.

Hadn't he said similar words, as he had sat on her sofa after ghosting her on their first date; that he wished they had met at a better time? She didn't interrupt and let him continue, holding onto the tree for support.

"I already told you what happened with Chantelle, about our argument, and that I had moved to the city to escape my broken past."

Carrie stared at him, unable to move, unable to blink; unable to do anything except listen.

"I really felt like I hadn't escaped my broken family life at that point, that I was making the same mistakes, attracting the same chaotic people into my life as the ones in my family. Namely my mother."

She felt her eyebrows rise and lowered them. "You were worried Chantelle was like your mum?"

He pressed his lips together and closed his eyes but said nothing.

"But you broke up with her. You met me. I'm different, if that's what you're worried about. I'm not alcoholic for a start and I would never use threats of suicide as an emotional weapon against you."

"I know that, and that's why this is so much more tragic than you think." His voice had a faded quality to it, as he trailed off.

Anger flooded her, as an image of Chantelle leaving their apartment building, carrying a large holdall bubbled through her veins. That had been a few days after the coffee date she'd had with Ken at the Coffee Lounge.

"What do you mean by tragic? Are you trying to break up with me? I saw Chantelle coming out of the lift in our building. You had spent the night with her. I didn't want to believe it at the time, but now I see that this is a pitiful excuse. Why don't you just be honest, Ken? You aren't dead. Why don't you just *say* that you got back with your ex? Why don't you just *admit* that you don't like me? Instead you tell me you're dead."

She shouted the last few words, unable to restrain her voice. Ken looked her square in the face and his broken expression almost melted her heart. Almost.

"I wish I could say you were right, but you aren't. I wish I could tell you that I cheated on you with my ex and that I was making a flimsy excuse to break up with you. Those reasons would be normal ones. But the truth is much stranger. I know this sounds incredible – even ridiculous – but what I've told you is real."

Carrie scoffed, rolling her eyes. "You aren't a ghost. I've felt you. I've done more than feel you."

He gave her a quizzical look. "Didn't you think anything was strange about our touch?"

What could be strange? She thought back to the first time she touched him, on her sofa, and how a cold electrical feeling had given her a static sting. The same with their first kiss. What about their night of passion? How he had felt so lightweight on top of her.

It all made sense. Too much sense. As everything slotted into place, her stomach began to twist into knots.

"Alright then, if you *really* are telling the truth and not giving some elaborate lie to cover up for getting back with Chantelle, then why did I see her leaving our apartment building a few days after our first date?"

Although Ken kept eye contact with her, his mouth turned downwards. "She was clearing out her things. My brother got her number from my phone and texted her to let her know I was dead. He texted everyone in my contacts list."

Carrie's suspicious mind kept working to find holes in his story. "Why didn't I get a text then?"

"You weren't in my contacts," Ken answered.

"But you texted me," she argued.

"I texted you, yes. But not with my physical body. I used the energy that I have in this form to send you messages." He swept his arms down his own body.

Messages from beyond the grave. She pushed the intrusive thoughts aside, still determined to catch him out.

"So, if you're really a ghost, then how did you die?"

He looked down at the grass, avoiding my gaze. "I took some pills on Valentine's Day. Actually, a lot of pills, washed down by the red wine that Chantelle and I were going to share – only we broke up. I started to get woozy, and the last thing I saw was the time on my clock as I fell asleep – it was at eleven thirty."

Her sceptical mind kept working overtime. "That can't be right. You came to my door at eleven thirty because you got the chocolates I left for you."

"I know it seems strange – it didn't make sense to me at first either. I woke up feeling amazing and then I found your chocolates on my doorstep. It made me feel on top of the world after all that I'd been through. I thought I had been given a second chance at life, and I felt thankful that the sleeping pills hadn't worked. But obviously I was wrong about that."

She shook her head, letting her upper lip curl. "No. You knocked on my door. How can a ghost knock?"

He shrugged. "I really can't say for sure. Maybe your love and care gave me a boost of energy that allowed my hand to rap on your door?"

Ghosts walk the earth until they finish what they have to do. Another intrusive thought, her brain betraying her. Scepticism changed to sickness as she began to understand. "If your ghost really knocked on my door on Valentine's Day, are you saying your body was lying, dead in your bed, the whole time when we had that conversation?"

He gulped. "Yes."

She began to shake and held firm to the tree to steady herself. "No. No, I don't believe it. This must be a dream. I must be asleep."

As if to confirm it wasn't a dream, Pippa let out a fearful cry in her cat carrier box.

"I'm afraid this is real," he said, his voice echoing.

She pointed a shaky finger at the headstone. "That's fake. It has to be. This is a practical joke, isn't it?"

But she couldn't deny their first coffee date, and how he hadn't touched his drink; how he had gone to the toilet and hadn't returned. "Is that why you didn't come back when you went to the toilet at the Coffee Lounge? You disappeared?"

"Yes," he answered. "I think, sharing all those intense emotions with you about my break-up with Chantelle burned through my energy. I wasn't able to replenish it until the next time I saw you. Believe me, I wanted to contact you sooner – to apologise – to let you know I cared. It tortured me to see you so upset thinking I had ghosted you."

"Though I guess the comparison was appropriate, considering the facts," she guffawed.

Laughing about it helped reduce Carrie's nerves and diminish the shaking. But when the laughter subsided, the rising sickness took hold in her chest again. "Did we really have sex, then? I mean, if you're actually a ghost, then you aren't even real."

"I *am* real, I'm just in a different form. Even though I'm not in a physical body anymore, it doesn't mean I'm *imagination*." There was a sarcastic edge to the last word. "I'm in spirit form now, pure energy."

Guilt nipped at her. "I'm sorry Ken. I didn't mean to be so callous. I don't know what's up with me."

He smiled. "I get it. It's natural to want to protect yourself from any hurt."

"Energy doesn't have any substance to it, though." She gripped Pippa's cat carrier tighter. "I'm just trying to make sense of it, that's all."

"Maybe I'm made of, you know, what's that substance ghosts are made of?" He flapped a hand in the air, thinking.

"Ectoplasm? Don't even ask me how I know that."

They both laughed. It felt lovely to share a happy moment together; especially if what he had to say was true – that he was dead.

"I guess that's how I was able to give you those roses. I think I made them 'manifest' from my own energy. It was almost like a magic trick in a way. Someone at my funeral had given me a posey of roses since I died on Valentine's Day. I was thinking of what to give you, for our dinner date, and then – suddenly – they appeared in my flat."

She shivered, thinking of the strange, rotten smell emanating from the roses in her flat. "Not the ones from your actual coffin?"

He shook his hands, quick to dismiss the suggestion. "No, just a manifestation of flowers that resembled the ones buried with me, since I thought it was a lovely gesture."

"What about the white chocolates you left? Were those a manifestation too?"

"That was different. I sent the message to my brother in a dream. He went and bought the present I asked him to get and left it for you."

It all made sense: how he had kept disappearing even though her flat remained locked; the cold electrical sensations when they touched; the strange shadows in her flat and how she had heard Ken's voice call her name.

He had been dead. A ghost. The whole time.

"We really *did* meet at a bad time. The worst." She sniffed and wiped tears away. "I think you're the love of my life, and now I can't even spend my life with you."

"I think I stayed on this earth to tell you that the past month with you has been the best time of my life," he said apologetically.

Or the best time of his death. "It has been the best time of mine too."

"But now I have to go. I'll wait for you up above – if that's where I get sent."

She nodded, and wiped another tear, unable to speak.

"I want you to know something, Carrie."

She closed her eyes, and let hot tears fall, soothing her cheeks.

"Know that for you, my answer is yes."

His voice, a fading echo.

"Know that I love you."

A Valentine's Day offer not meant to be.

"I love you."

White Day whispers.

"I love you too, Ken." She opened her eyes and blew a kiss into nothingness. It was her, and Pippa, in the empty, moonlit graveyard.

2

Stone cold heart

Four hundred and fifty pounds a month for a room in a house share. Sebastian scratched his head.

"I thought the ad said it was three hundred and seventy-five?"

Tyreese, the tenant who was showing him the house, stroked his chin in thought. "We lost one of our friends in the middle of the tenancy, so we need to sublet at a higher rate to make up the cost. Is it not doable for you?"

Sebastian looked around at the furnishings. It was a cosy house, and well-maintained. Not to mention the fact that Tyreese was very attractive, with his golden-brown skin, curly hair and dazzling smile. No time to get distracted though. "Why did the other tenant leave?"

Tyreese avoided his eye for the first time since he had arrived for the tour. "Something came up. Listen, if it's not manageable, there's this other bloke who's coming to see it at ten."

High pressure tactics. Tyreese and the other tenant, Colm, must have been desperate. He needed to think on the spot. The house was in a good location, so that would save commuting costs, and Tyreese seemed like a quiet, introverted sort. Probably better to take his own hard stance. "You definitely don't have people around to visit? I mean, your ad said you wanted a quiet professional. I'm not up for even the occasional party."

"That won't be a problem. Colm and I both work so much our time off doesn't really sync up. We try to do movie nights occasionally, or when Jack was here, we played cards on Saturdays–" Tyreese faltered, his mouth hanging open for a moment before he composed himself.

Money would be tight for a while, but Sebastian couldn't think where he might find cheaper rent. "Alright then, I'm in. As long as the rent stays at four fifty, that works for me."

Tyreese grinned broadly. "Brilliant. I'll give you my bank details to transfer the payment, as I handle the standing order for the house, and you can move in whenever you're ready. The room is free."

***

Sebastian yawned and stretched. The mattress was more comfortable than it had seemed at first glance. He had slept well for his first night in the house share.

Colm had seemed as nice as Tyreese when he had bumped into him in the kitchen, earlier that morning. He had gone downstairs for a glass of water, and Colm had arrived back from a nightshift at the supermarket where he worked in the stockroom.

Tyreese had already left for work at the station café where he was a barrista. Sebastian's bedroom was at the front of the house, and he had heard Tyreese leaving just before eight o'clock. With Colm snoring away in the room opposite his, that meant the bathroom would be free. Sharing a house would take a while to get used to; he would have to plan showering and cooking times around his new house mates.

As Sebastian stepped out onto the landing, holding his shaving bag, he noticed a shadow pass into the bathroom before the door swung shut.

That was strange. Colm's snoring was louder than ever as he stood on the landing. Had he made a mistake about Tyreese leaving? Maybe Tyreese had forgot something and had come home. That might explain it; maybe he had been half asleep and hadn't heard the door opening again.

He turned back into his bedroom, but left the door ajar so he could hear when Tyreese finished. Sebastian glanced at his clock radio. Eight fifteen. He needed to be ready for his shift at the apothecary for nine thirty. If Tyreese took too long, he would be cutting it fine.

The bathroom door clicked open. Sebastian whipped himself off the bed, where he had been perched, and dashed for the landing as a flash of blonde hair went into the room next to the bathroom, beside Colm's room.

Huh? Wasn't that the empty bedroom where the other tenant had stayed? That's what Tyreese had explained on the house tour; Sebastian would take the empty room at the front opposite Colm's, and he had the back bedroom next to the bathroom, on the other side of Jack's old room.

He shrugged to himself as he padded along the landing. Maybe Colm had arranged a fourth tenant and hadn't yet told Tyreese. He hoped so; if there were four of them, that would bring the rent down.

There was a lingering cold in the bathroom as he entered. Sebastian shivered. Maybe the lads had been short on heating, since Jack had left the picture, and it *was* early February after all. He cranked up the heating on the electric shower to max and let the blast of steam rid him of goosebumps. What would eleven hundred and twenty-five quid be, divided by four house mates? Two eighty a month? Sweet. That would be *sweet*. Whoever the blonde bloke was, the new tenant was an angel.

***

"What are you making?"

His question caused Tyreese to spin, cooking spoon in hand. "Just spag bol. Nothing fancy."

Sebastian's eyes landed on Tyreese's novelty apron, showing a cartoon female body with large breasts, wearing only black underwear. He chortled. "Nice look."

Tyreese was bashful. "Christmas present from Colm. He calls me the house mum as I'm the only one who cooks properly. He's a frozen pizza man."

"I'm not much better." Sebastian showed the two frozen chicken kievs that he had picked up from the convenience store on the corner. "Your food smells great. Sure beats my dinner."

Tyreese flashed one of his gorgeous grins. "You're welcome to join me, if you like? I made a bit too much anyway. I usually leave it for Colm, but he never wants to eat when he gets back at five in the morning, so it always solidifies in the pan. You wouldn't *believe* the number of pots we've gone through in two years living together."

Sebastian chuckled. "Alright then, you're on. I'd love some."

Tyreese dished out two servings and set them on the small kitchen table. He took off his saucy apron and hooked it on the door, then sat opposite Sebastian to eat.

"This is delicious. You're an amazing cook," he said between mouthfuls. After finishing his meal, he wiped his mouth on the back of his hand, and ran his tongue over his teeth; why was he so conscious of needing to look good for Tyreese?

Tyreese beamed. "Well, I'm glad someone appreciates my food, at last."

"Colm doesn't know what he's missing." Sebastian filled the sink with hot soapy water and started washing the dishes.

"It's good to have company in the house too. Colm only ever works nights, so it's usually just me here, talking to myself." Tyreese snorted.

"Well, you won't be lonely any more with me and the other tenant in the house."

Silence filled the room. As the pause continued, Sebastian turned around.

"Have you met the other tenant?"

Tyreese frowned. "What other tenant?"

Sebastian hesitated. "The blonde-haired bloke in the bedroom next to Colm's."

Tyreese's mouth fell open. He closed it and swallowed.

"Maybe Colm didn't tell you yet, if you say he's so busy?"

Tyreese shook his head. "There is no other tenant. Not yet anyway. The man who came to see the house after you, Scott, changed his mind after I showed him the last room. He didn't say why, he just didn't call me back."

Sebastian's mind wandered to the man he had seen upstairs. "I definitely saw a man with floppy blonde hair going onto the other room this morning."

Tyreese stood up from the kitchen table. He was pale. "You must have been dreaming."

Why was Tyreese suddenly so closed off?

"Well…" Sebastian sighed. "I mean, it's *possible*, I suppose, thought I don't see how. I was wide awake."

"I have indigestion. I think I'm going to go and lie down," said Tyreese, a pained expression on his face.

What was going on?

***

Sebastian glugged the glassful of water down in one go and refilled it. There was a full moon outside that threw a silvery sheen over the back courtyard where the row of houses shared communal dumpsters. Shame there wasn't a proper garden. An image of Tyreese barbecuing a hotdog sausage, among English roses, wearing his novelty apron floated into his mind. In his musings, he stood next to Tyreese, ready to catch the delicious, thick, brown sausage in a white floury bun.

Hands sliding around his middle from behind distracted Sebastian from his fantasy. His jolt of surprise turned to one of excitement as he felt the tickle of breath on his neck, and felt a tingle as lips kissed under his jaw.

"Tyreese," he whispered, his heart racing.

As blonde hair fell forward over his shoulder, Sebastian let out a yelp and spun around. The glass tumbled from his hand and smashed on the kitchen tiles.

Nobody was there.

The landing light switched on and a moment later, a flurry of feet on the stairs sounded as Tyreese hurried into the kitchen, wearing checkered green shorts and a tight-fitting grey t-shirt that showed off his slender abdomen and broad shoulders. He flicked the kitchen light on and the glow illuminated his wide, dark eyes.

"What happened?"

Sebastian gulped and said nothing.

Tyreese's eyes dropped to the smashed glass. "Why were you down here in the dark?"

His voice suddenly returned. "I was thirsty. I was getting a quick glass of water."

"You should've turned on the light," Tyreese scolded.

"I didn't drop it because of the dark." He swallowed again, trying to compose his thoughts.

Tyreese peered at him, his face full of worry. "Are you sure you're okay?"

Irritation nipped at him. "I'm fine. I had a weird experience just now. I'm a bit freaked out, honestly."

Tyreese folded his arms. "What kind of weird experience?"

Sebastian raised his chin to bolster his confidence. "I, well. I swear the blonde man I saw yesterday was in here a few minutes ago and–"

Tyreese's face fell. He didn't prompt him to continue, but Sebastian did, regardless.

"And he kissed my neck. It was like, he was making his way around to my face."

Tyreese looked visibly ill. Nauseous. As though he might vomit. He gave a nervous laugh. "Did someone put you up to this? I don't think it's funny."

"What are you talking about?"

Tyreese took a step backwards, framed in the kitchen doorway. "You must have known Jack."

"Jack? You mean, the last tenant? The one who left?" said Sebastian. "I didn't know Jack. What's going on?"

Tyreese hugged himself, rubbing his arms for warmth. Sebastian sat down at the kitchen table. Whatever Tyreese had to say didn't seem good, judging by his demeanour.

"I met Colm and Jack when they were regular customers in my café, and we became friends. We decided to get a house share together, as HMO houses are just too expensive. In order to get a house together, Colm and I pretended to be brothers, as coincidentally we both have the same surname: Foster. Colm's mum was happy to be our guarantor for the house, so the estate agent didn't ask too many questions about why we wanted a four-bed property – so long as they were getting their rent."

Tyreese took a deep breath and continued. "Jack moved in with us too, of course, and we were all three friends – at first. Just before Valentine's Day last year, Jack and I realised our feelings for each other. We kept it from Colm for a while, so he wouldn't feel awkward, but it turned out he didn't care. That bloke is all work, work, work."

Tyreese steadied himself with his shoulder against the door jamb. "I knew that Jack had wandering eyes when we went out for dinner, or drinks, but I didn't think anything of it. He was working as a model, and was taking home lots of cash, so we never had problems paying the rent."

Sebastian braced himself. "What happened?"

"Colm saw him when he was finishing one of his night shifts. He had his arm around another man, leaving an all-night club, practically legless."

"Is that why he left here? Because you caught him cheating and kicked him out?"

"Kind of." Tyreese's voice saddened. "We all got into an argument. I felt betrayed by him, and he felt betrayed by Colm. He left of his own accord."

"But that's a good thing, isn't it? You got rid of a cheater, and now you can have a fresh start," Sebastian said.

"It's not so simple. Jack apparently went on a bender after our break-up. I think he had never been dumped before. He tried to cross the train tracks after he left the station bar while he was hammered, and–" Tyreese closed his eyes, and tears streamed over his cheeks. That happened last summer."

"Oh, shit." Sebastian strode across to Tyreese. Without thinking, he wrapped him in his arms, letting him sob into his chest.

As Tyreese cried, Sebastian mulled over what he had just heard. If Jack was dead, did that mean, he was back to haunt the house? The place where he had spent so many happy – and strong emotions?

Tyreese's tears subsided and he wiped his face. "Jack had paid his share of rent in advance for the rest of last year from his modelling work. Our tenancy was renewed in January, and the rent went up. That's why we had to ask you for more, to cover the cost. Only until we find a fourth tenant – that is, if you still want to stay too, after what I've told you."

Sebastian blinked at Tyreese. "Why wouldn't I want to stay?"

"Because of Jack's ghost." He sniffed away more tears. "I'll be honest, I've seen him once or twice myself. He's becoming clearer as we get closer to the anniversary of our first official date – on Valentine's Day."

Sebastian forced his brain into action. He had to help. He wanted to help. "None of what happened was your fault. Jack chose to cheat on you. He chose to get drunk and what happened with the train was a horrible accident. Do you still love him? Is that why you're sad?"

"No." Tyreese's answer was quick, defensive. "I suppose it was never love. I was besotted by him. I don't think he cared about me."

"I'm sorry you went through all that," Sebastian added.

Tyreese gave him a weak smile, his eyes still watery. *But, I care about you.*

Sebastian didn't speak his mind. Instead, he said, "I have an idea. A plan for how to rid this house of Jack's ghost."

***

Sebastian set the pink ceramic heart on the floor of the empty bedroom. It was a money bank, now placed in the room that had once been so important to Jack. He held the sage incense stick in one hand and a lighter in the other.

Tyreese eyed him from the doorway, one dubious eyebrow tilted upwards. "What's all this for?"

Sebastian gave him a reassuring smile. "You'll see."

He lit the incense stick and wafted the scented smoke in all four corners of the room. He billowed it over the bed, wardrobe and chest of drawers, then streamed it across the window, doorway and over the floor. The swirling smoke pooled in the centre of the room. Sebastian observed the smoke as it sank towards the money-bank. Tyreese gasped as he watched too. The smoke highlighted a spectral form that otherwise would have remained invisible; floppy hair framing handsome features. Although faint, Jack remained unmarred by death.

"Jack. My name is Sebastian. I know that my presence in this house brought you back. You sensed a change in the house share, and it made you jealous, didn't it?"

The ghost tried to speak, but couldn't; the cleansing sage from the apothecary where he worked was doing its job.

"Today is Valentine's Day. I know that this should have been your anniversary with Tyreese, but it wasn't to be. You made your choices, and you need to accept the consequences of your actions."

More silent complaints from Jack's ghostly lips.

"This house isn't yours any longer. It belongs to Tyreese, and to Colm, and to me."

More protestations, unheard.

"I am in this house now, and I am with Tyreese, and you need to accept that, for we're doing it with your blessing – or not."

Jack stopped trying to protest and lowered his chin. The incense smoke coiled around him and began pulling him towards the slot in the centre of the ceramic heart. His ghostly body began diminishing into a wisp and drifting inside the slot. Once there was no more trace of neither smoke nor spectre, Sebastian pushed the incense stick into the slot and blew out the glowing tip.

"Is he gone?"

"Yes. He couldn't move on, and he wanted to haunt us, rather than see you happy with anyone else. I've sealed him inside this heart where he can't hurt you anymore."

"What are you going to do with the heart?"

Sebastian concentrated. "I know. I'll donate it to the Station bar where you said he was drinking that night. They have all sorts of interesting nicknacks on their shelves. It'll be a shrine to honour his death."

One corner of Tyreese's mouth tugged upwards. "I suppose it's fitting. A stone cold heart for a doomed romance."

"Well, you've got a red-pumping heart right here." Sebastian strode over to Tyreese and kissed him. "Four hundred and fifty pounds a month for a house share? Worth every penny!"

3

Violets are Blue

The bell on the charity shop door tinkled as Angela opened it and stepped inside. The smell of vintage clothes hit her nostrils as she slipped through the aisles and scanned the racks. She needed something cheap, but classy, that still looked new. Christmas had hit her finances harder than she would have liked, and Stephen's birthday was coming up the day before Valentine's Day. He was her line manager, so going out for a work shindig that combined his birthday with all-things-romance had become an obligatory date on the 13th February since the previous year, but she enjoyed it, besides. Stephen was pretty cute, in a nerdy way. With his light brown hair, wide-set, deep blue eyes and thick-framed glasses, he pulled off the Maths-dork look perfectly, and many of the office girls had cast an eye his way over the eighteen months since he'd joined the team.

A pair of blue, velvet trousers jumped out at her from one of the pegs. They were straight-legged, but didn't look like they would cling too much. She wanted to look casually elegant, so anything too form-fitting would make her look desperate, but anything too baggy wouldn't compete with the likes of Sheree, who no doubt would wear a barely-there dress, or Maggie, whose voluptuous form and impressive bust were always eye-catching.

Angela held the trousers against her body and looked in the full-length shop mirror. Looked good so far, and definitely worth trying on. They had a charm that she couldn't put her finger on. Maybe it was the sheen, allowing them to catch the light in different ways. Or maybe it was the soft fluffiness of the fabric, which gave the comfort of pyjamas while still looking glamorous.

She slipped into the fitting room and removed her cargo jeans. The velvet trousers seemed to flow over her skin like water as she pulled them up her shins, over her knees and along her thighs. She wasn't sure if their colour would clash with her shoulder-length dyed burgundy curls, but she didn't care. They had an allure that she couldn't resist.

Angela turned to one side, admiring the line of the trousers on her legs, then turned to look in the mirror and see behind. They were tight on her behind and thighs, then loose below the knee, giving an almost bootcut look.

Perfect.

***

Angela lay on the sofa, munching from a giant bag of caramel popcorn that lay on her stomach. Her pyjamas were covered in sticky crumbs.

A flash of bright blue drew her attention to her new trousers, which she had left dangling over the armchair backrest, as soon as she had got home. *Wowee,* they sure could catch the light; there was barely any sunshine on such a dreary day, yet the velvety sheen of her lucky charity shop find grabbed all her focus. If they could steal her focus away from the TV, what would they do for Stephen's attention at the party?

She paused the show she was watching, stood up and dusted crumbs off herself. Too much of the single life and she was turning into a slob. Her pyjamas could do with a wash. She pulled off her bottoms, tossed them on the floor, and grabbed the blue, velvet trousers off the armchair. Even as she slipped them on, a tingling sensation prickled her skin; that had to be the excitement she felt at the thought of wearing something so sleek and sexy – and unlike herself – to the forthcoming party.

Had an item of clothing ever made her feel so seductive before? She pondered the thought as she spun, watching her reflection in the paused TV. No, not ever before. It wasn't that she felt unattractive; just that she cared about other things more than how she looked. Until now, of course. Why did it matter that she should look more attractive to Stephen than

Sheree, or Maggie? Such things were trivial, weren't they?

It was the trousers. Something about them gave her a tantalising thrill; a dangerous excitement at the thought of flirting with Stephen. And not just *flirting* with him. Seducing him.

Angela resumed her place on the sofa, but this time she sat upright with proper poise, instead of slouching like normal. Her thighs looked so much slimmer in tight-fitting clothing rather than hidden from view in baggy, shapeless jeans. Even at home with only herself to impress, she felt elegant in a way she didn't normally.

She un-paused the TV and resumed delving into her big bag of popcorn. The neckline of her top felt restrictive as she ate, so she tugged to loosen it with her index finger. After only a few more handfuls of popcorn, her top seemed to have tightened and was cutting into her throat again.

It was her velvet trousers. The fabric was gripping the cotton material and tugging on it, like Velcro.

Not a problem. Maybe a synthetic fabric like her blue velvet trousers needed to be matched with other synthetic fibres. She had just the top in mind for Stephen's birthday party; a slippery and sleek, black spandex top. It was figure-hugging too, so a good combination with the dazzling blue bottoms.

For now, she also needed a synthetic fabric instead of cotton. Angela whipped off her pyjama top and strode to the bedroom to get changed. She found a satin teddy in the back of her wardrobe that hadn't been worn since she'd last had a bloke to impress, but the convenience factor was a good enough reason to bring it out of storage in the meantime.

Back to her show, with hopefully no more interruptions. She foraged for the last remaining scraps of popcorn at the bottom of the bag and tucked in, her legs crossed on the sofa and bag wedged between.

An oppressive warmth began to flood her upper body. At first, it started as prickly heat that tingled her shoulders and crept across her upper chest, before spreading along her core and radiating up into her neck and face. She had no choice but to strip off her new trousers and old teddy, finishing the show in only her underwear. Immediately the heat dissipated.

Weird-o-rama. Maybe she was coming down with a nasty cold, or other viral infection. Not unexpected in the middle of flu season, after all, and nothing that a few days of rest wouldn't fix.

Angela folded the trousers and set them on the armchair. A few days off work would be enough time to rest before Stephen's bash; and then, fingers crossed, she would make an impression.

***

Saturday night. Angela was thankful that Daisy had suggested a pre-party drink at the bar of the restaurant where they would be meeting for Stephen's party. It was a good idea for two reasons: first, some liquor for confidence. Second, she wouldn't have to walk into the party by herself.

Angela slipped among the throng and spotted her friend taking a G&T she had just ordered from the barman. Daisy was wearing a lime green lanna dress that cut below her knees with vintage glass buttons. The look suited her black bob and red glasses creating bold colours; conservative but fun. Angela enjoyed the feel of her velvet trousers as she sashayed into the pub, feeling daring in comparison, and wondering what her work-friend would think of the change in her appearance.

Daisy peered over the rim of her red framed glasses. "Ooh, Angela, look at you? Where did you get those amazing trousers?"

"What, these old things? I've had them for ages, just decided that tonight's party was a good chance to get them out of the wardrobe."

Why did she feel the need to lie to Daisy, and about something so trivial? She felt her forehead crease and relaxed her brow. Daisy's attention had moved onto her hair, tugging on her curly mane.

"I swear you look like a completely different person, so glam." Daisy puckered her mouth. "That's not to say you don't *always* look great, of course."

Angela grinned. "I knew what you meant. But you're right, I'm normally so casual, and even a bit grungy. This makes for a change."

Her attention diverted behind Daisy's shoulder as Stephen walked in. He was wearing a short-sleeved black polo shirt with blue jeans and brown suede ankle boots. Very sexy indeed. She pushed her chest out and bent the knee of one leg, making the light shimmer on the blue velvet of her trousers.

Stephen smiled when he saw them and opened his arms wide. "Hey, you two are starting early!"

His eyes dropped to Angela's legs; the outcome she was hoping for with her eye-catching outfit. His gaze travelled up the line of her leg and, every bit the sophisticated gent, skipped upwards to her face without settling on her cleavage. *Nice.* Not only gorgeous, but classy too. She approved.

"Can I get you ladies a drink?"

Daisy batted his arm. "Don't be silly, it's your birthday. What can we get for you?"

"I'll get this round, you've already got your drink." Angela nodded to Daisy's Gin and Tonic. "What'll it be?"

"I'll start with a pint of Abbot, please," he said.

Just in the nick of time; Sheree and Maggie strutted into the foyer of the restaurant. Lucky that she had got her order in before they came along and doubled what she would be have to spend on a round. She was happy to buy for Stephen, Daisy and herself, but those office loud-mouths were fake friends, at best. As expected, Sheree wore a skin coloured bodycon dress that cut under her gym-honed backside and skimmed low over her chest, while Maggie's ample rack was sticking out to maximum effect in a black corset dress with a skirt that was split to the thigh.

"Here comes the tart brigade," Daisy whispered. Angela snickered behind her hand.

A tug on the back of her trousers made Angela turn. Was that Sheree, or Maggie being annoying? Mild irritation gave way to confusion; nobody was there. Her velvet trousers had definitely slipped down, no matter the reason. She adjusted them and turned back to rest her elbows on the bar, while waiting for their order.

Heat began to trickle from her hairline, seeping across her face and down into her neck and chest. Maybe the bar was too hot. She fanned herself with one hand. Again, a slight tug on the back waistband of her trousers drew her attention to them and she yanked them up with one hand. There was always a catch; if they were prone to slipping down, maybe that was the reason why their previous owner had donated them to a charity shop.

The barman set their drinks on the counter and Angela leaned across to reach for them; as she did so, her black satin vest top rode up as the velvet trousers tugged downwards once more. From the corner of her eye, she saw Stephen take a sneaky peek of the rim of her lace thong, which had poked out over the top of her low-riding trousers. She shouldn't have second-guessed her charity stop buy after all; blue velvet trousers for the win.

***

Double win. After an amazing party, during which an evening of flirting with Stephen had led to them dancing together, then sharing a taxi together, followed by 'coffee' at her place, Angela rolled her head to her left to see Stephen sleeping soundly in her bed beside her. Technically that meant she wasn't single, and on Valentine's Day no less. The morning sunlight streamed through a gap in the curtain, allowing her ample light to admire his bare chest rising and falling in his slumber, his mouth slightly parted. How on *earth* had she managed to pull her boss? For the past eighteen months, she had tried flirting while they had lingered over the photocopier, or while waiting for the kettle to boil in the office kitchen. He had always been pleasant and polite when rebuffing her subtle advances; so, what was the difference now? It wasn't alcohol; at least, she didn't *think* it was. The team had been out to the pub a few times over the past year and a half, and both of them had been more intoxicated on those occasions than they had the previous evening, yet nothing had ever happened before.

Angela rolled her head to the right, and gazed upon the blue velvet trousers, which were lying on the floor where Stephen had stripped them off in a passionate frenzy the night before. Yes, they accentuated the shape of her legs; but was that enough to seduce her boss?

Stephen's eyelashes fluttered. He stared at her with eyelids half-shut for a couple of seconds, then blinked his eyes wide open. A look of horror traversed his face before he sat bolt upright and stared down at her.

"Angela," he gasped.

"Good morning," she said, in her sexiest purr.

Stephen clutched the bed sheet around himself, covering his bare chest and draping it down over the rest of his naked body. He swung his legs over the side of hand and turned to face her, still bunching the bed sheet over himself with one hand, and stooped to grab his clothes off the floor with the other hand.

"This was a—" His face flushed bright red. "—Listen, I'll see you at the office."

This was a mistake. She filled in the word in her head as she watched him back out of the room. Her bathroom door slammed shut, then a few minutes later, clicked open and she heard a flurry of feet going down her stairs. The sound of the front door opening and clicking firmly shut suggested that Stephen had left her house.

What was with that? Bewilderment gave way to embarrassment and finally anger. Even if he *was* her boss, he had been so rude about the whole situation. There was no need to act like a pompous ass, especially to a junior colleague, even if it had only been a meaningless one-night stand. She cast another glance at her blue velvet trousers. It seemed they had proved to be unlucky after all. It had turned out to be the *worst* Valentine's Day that she'd ever had.

***

Work on Monday was awkward in a way it had never been before. Angela chose a grey polka-dot dress, smart but not attention-grabbing in any way, and kept her head down around her colleagues. She half-expected a barrage of questions, which kept running through her mind:

Well? I saw you dancing with the boss. Pray tell?

Where did you and Stephen sneak off to in that taxi?

Did you get up to anything fun with the boss after you left in a hurry?

Fanciful thoughts, yet nothing came of it. Sheree gave her a frosty look, and Maggie was distant and formal, implying that both suspected she'd shagged the boss, but nobody asked a thing.

The worst moment came much later in the day. She finally finished a report she had been working on all week. Stephen had requested that she print it for him to proofread before he needed to submit it to the company investors. Why, of all days, did she have to submit the report right *after* their one-night stand at the weekend?

Her mind drifted again to the blue trousers, full of thoughts of how sexy she had been in their lush velvet fabric at the weekend. More so after Stephen didn't even raise his eyes to meet hers when she entered his office, simply giving a grunt of acknowledgement when she dropped the report on his desk. Maybe tomorrow, she would wear the velvet trousers and let them work their intoxicating magic on him.

Her thoughts stayed on the trousers for the rest of the afternoon. She couldn't wait to get home and give them another try; to feel their electrifying energy on her skin. Was it normal to feel so obsessed with an item of clothing? Probably not, but it was a harmless fixation, and most likely only temporary too, until her next shopping spree.

As soon as she got home, Angela waited no longer. The sensation as she slipped the trousers on was like sliding into a warm bath. She closed her eyes and revelled in the bliss.

Behind her closed eyelids, an image appeared. A young, slim, blonde-haired woman wore the blue velvet trousers as she watched her reflection in a full-length mirror. The woman turned to the left, then the right, with a satisfied smile on her face. A man stood behind her, grinning at her delight. The woman threw her arms around his neck and embraced him.

Violet. The woman's name was Violet.

Angela opened her eyes. What a kooky daydream. What on earth put such a thought into her head?

It couldn't have been real, could it? There was no way it was a memory belonging to the former owner of her trousers, was it? No way could such a thing be possible. Fair enough, she had heard of second-hand engagement rings harbouring energy from their former owners; but never clothing.

She had been so wrapped up in the daydream that she didn't notice the constriction on her neck. The neckline of her top was cutting into the skin on her throat as the velvet trousers pulled at the hem, causing the fabric to snag on her back.

What an annoying drawback; the only she had found so far about her charity shop buy. But it was a significant one; possibly even a *big* enough drawback that she might have to reserve wearing the trousers for only special occasions.

Angela cast a downward glance at the trousers. They were so sleek and lovely, and they gave her silhouette a sleek elegance that boosted her confidence. Such a bonus overrode any negative aspects, like how they tugged on the fabric of her tops, causing them to constrict her neck. She looked almost as good in the trousers as the blonde-haired woman from her daydream. Violet. Real or imagined, the woman from her musings was Violet.

***

"Oh boy, I *do* love those trousers. I noticed them at dinner on Saturday, but didn't get a chance to say how good they look on you."

Angela turned to see who was behind her in the office kitchen. "Oh, thanks. You're Ruby from accounts, aren't you?"

"That's right. I've seen you around so much and didn't realise we hadn't officially met. I know it's a big company, but still, how awkward." The red-haired woman chortled. "Yes, I'm Ruby. What's your name again?"

"Violet," said Angela.

"That's a lovely name, very unusual," said Ruby.

Angela jolted to her senses. "What am I saying, oh my gosh? My name's Angela, not Violet."

Ruby gave a bemused grin. "Well, Angela is nice too."

How on earth was she going to explain such an awkward slip? "Erm, Violet is my middle name. Some people in my family call me by it instead of Angela."

"Which do you prefer, then?" said Ruby.

She hated lying. Time to end the conversation before she dug herself an even bigger hole. "Angela. Not Violet at all. Just Angela."

Violet. Angela tossed her head as she stirred the milk in her tea. She had to forget about the blonde-haired woman who had invaded her thoughts the previous day when she put the trousers on. Real or imagined, Violet was becoming an unwelcome addition to her thoughts.

She walked past her office towards Stephen's at the end of the corridor. Wonder what he wanted to discuss with her about the draft report she had printed for him?

As she entered his office, Stephen looked up from her report on his desk with a stoic intensity. His serious expression dissipated into a dreamy daze the moment he set eyes on her blue, velvet trousers. His gaze travelled up the length of her legs in a slow, hypnotic motion and by the time his eyes met hers, a heavy, brooding lust settled across his face.

"Erm, you wanted to see me about my report?" she said.

He swept her report aside with one hand. "That's not important right now."

Her eyebrows shot upwards. "Oh-kay? I thought there might be an issue you wanted me to fix?"

"It can wait." He walked around the side of his desk. "I wanted to apologise for Sunday morning. I left, in such a hurry."

Heat flooded her cheeks. "Oh! Um, that's okay. I'm sure you had a good reason."

He shook his head. "I didn't. That's why I'm saying sorry."

Angela tucked a strand of hair behind her ear as she thought of what to say. "Well, thank you. I appreciate the apology."

What was with his complete attitude change? He had gone from being completely aloof, bordering on rude, to flirtatious. And, *Wowee*, he was so sexy.

Stephen strode across the room and clicked the lock on his door. He swivelled around, and in one swift move, hooked one hand around behind her waist and ran the other through her hair as he pulled her close. As his lips met her mouth, a tingle flooded downwards, heating every part of her body.

As their kiss became more passionate, they stumbled backwards until she felt his desk bump against her backside. Stephen ran his hands up and down the soft fabric of her velvet trousers before he tugged on them, sliding them down. Angela lay back across her discarded report, as he pulled her trousers and underwear down until they dangled on only one ankle.

What followed was a hard and fast flurry of sweaty sex. Her report was crumpled, Stephen's pen holder had scattered on the floor, and her heart raced faster than ever. Was her infatuation with her boss becoming more serious? Her new trousers gave her a confidence boost that made her feel she could do anything: achieve what she wanted; get any man she wanted. Right now, she only had eyes for one. If she didn't love Stephen before, she certainly did now.

"My report," she laughed. "It's wrecked."

"Don't worry about it," he said, in between heavy breaths. "I'll fix it."

"You're sure? If you tell me what needs amending, I can do it by the end of the day."

He shook his head. "You're not getting away so soon."

Round two. What bliss was this? If there was a heaven, then surely, this was it.

***

Violet baby, you look so hot. Your ass is so sexy in those trousers.

The blonde woman turned on the spot, showing off her curves in the blue, velvet trousers.

Just as suddenly as she had appeared, the woman disappeared, and Angela was left with a lingering feeling of jealousy at how good she looked in the blue, velvet trousers.

Mental shake up: what on earth?

Jealousy evaporated, leaving confusion to fill the void. It hadn't been a daydream this time. The blonde woman, Violet, had actually appeared in the reflection of her kitchen window. The man's voice, calling her 'hot' and 'sexy' tickled her ears as though he had been right there, in her kitchen, speaking the words to her.

Angela clapped a hand against her chest to calm herself. What was going on? If it wasn't a daydream, then what? A lucid dream? But she wasn't asleep either.

Coldness descended and she gulped as goosebumps besieged her whole body. Violet couldn't possibly be a—

No, that was silly. She dismissed the thought.

Angela's chin dropped to her chest, and she peered down the length of her body at the blue, velvet trousers. She grabbed the waistline with both hands and whipped them off, leaving them in a pile on the floor.

The first time she had seen the image of Violet in her mind, and had entertained the notion that the trousers were harbouring memories of their past owner, it hadn't occurred to her that Violet could be dead. If the images really were Violet's ghost, then that changed her feelings about the trousers entirely. They would have to go straight back to the charity shop tomorrow.

Mind you…

She studied the shimmering pile in front of her on the floor. On the other hand, they had been entirely responsible for her success in the romance department with Stephen. In eighteen months of flirtatious office banter, she hadn't managed to seduce him, and in the space of three days had enjoyed sex with her boss three times. Even the thought stirred her libido in a groin-tingling way like nothing else could. If Violet was a ghost, then as long as she wasn't a *harmful* ghost, the trousers could stay.

***

"Angela, is it true?"

Angela kept her face glued to her computer screen. Whoever was speaking behind her must've been talking to someone else.

"Hello, wakey wakey. Angela?"

A nudge on her shoulder. She pressed her lips together and turned to look over her left shoulder. A woman with a black bob, heavy fringe and red glasses stood behind her.

"What is *with* you today?" said the woman.

Angela frowned. "Are you talking to me?"

The woman folded her arms across her chest. "Are you sure you're alright? You didn't hit your head or something?"

"I'm sorry, you must have mistaken me for someone else." Angela turned back to her computer.

The woman made a noise of exasperation behind her. "What-ev. Be an ignoramus then. I'll go and get you a coffee and maybe you can apologise to me later."

A few minutes later, she heard her office door open and the woman returned. She set a mug of coffee down on her desk and perched her bottom next to Angela's mouse.

"Alright then, care to explain what's going on? What's with all the rudeness? It's not because you don't want people to know you shagged the boss? Well love, the cat's already out of the bag with that one, as the whole building knows."

Who was this rude woman and what was she on about? "I'm sorry, who are you?"

The black-haired woman's eyes became owlish behind her red glasses. "Sheesh, Angela, would you drop the act already, it isn't even funny."

"Who's Angela? I'm Violet." Angela spun in her swivel chair and faced the black-haired woman, then rubbed both palms on her blue velvet trousers.

The black-haired woman's face scrunched up. "Who's Violet?"

It was as if a veil mysteriously lifted. Angela recognised her friend Daisy, roving her with suspicion. "Daisy? Did you just say something?"

Daisy continued watching her, unblinking, with her arms still folded. "Are you okay? Do you need to go home and lie down?"

A wave of nausea rippled over Angela, followed by another, and one more. On the third, she retched, her stomach convulsing, but no vomit came out, only dry heaves.

"I don't know what's wrong with me. Maybe I'm coming down with a stomach bug," Angela gasped.

Daisy shook her head. "You said your name was Violet."

Violet. A cold sweat broke out all over Angela's body.

Was Violet trying to possess her?

***

Angela walked past the shop fronts on the high street, most still decorated with heart-themed displays from Valentine's Day the previous week. She caught sight of her reflection in one of the windows, her long, blonde-hair streaming over her shoulders in the wind.

She did a double take. Gone was Violet's blonde hair, replaced by her own curly, dyed burgundy barnet.

Her breath came in short rasps, as her heart hammered, and her lungs expelled the air from her chest.

What was going on? She wasn't even wearing the blue, velvet–

Angela glanced down her body and made a gagging noise.

Since when had she put on the blue velvet ones? The last thing she recalled was putting on a pair of beige and brown checkered trousers before leaving her house. Could she have changed at the last minute and had a memory blackout? If Violet really *was* possessing her, then maybe she had done it unconsciously.

Momentary madness – or a stroke of genius – seized her. First she looked left, then right, to check that she was alone in the post-rush hour street. Using her long winter coat as cover, Angela whipped the blue trousers down. She balanced with one hand against the shop window and pulled the leg off one ankle, then the other, slipping her feet back into her sheepskin boots in turn. The charity shop was still open until five thirty. She had seven minutes to get rid of the trousers. Time for them to go.

Angela left the trousers with the shop staff at the counter. As she turned to walk home, she felt a great weight lift off her shoulders. It was the right decision. Besides, they had served their usefulness; she'd had the best Valentine's Day and had even shagged Stephen in his own office; memories that wouldn't soon fade from her mind, even if they weren't to be repeated.

When she got home, Angela kicked off her winter boots and hung her coat on the peg by the door. She went upstairs in her socks and knickers, wearing only her red woollen jumper. It gave her a giggle to think of what she had done, stripping off her bottoms in public, even if it had been a deserted street. Must have been Violet's influence one last time to make her abandon reason for madness, but she didn't regret the decision to get rid of the velvet trousers.

She flicked on her bedroom light, ready to grab her pyjamas, and stopped dead in her tracks.

The blue velvet trousers lay in a neatly folded pile at the foot of her bed.

Angela's hands flew to her cheeks and a strangled scream choked out of her mouth.

How was that possible? How could the trousers have not only left the charity shop by themselves, but made it back to her home before she did? She took a cautious step towards them, and another, then another and snatched them off the bed.

A wave of anger consumed her. With a roar of fury, Angela gripped the elastic waistband in both hands and stretched her arms apart. A ripping noise sounded as the threads tore. She gripped one of the velvet legs in her teeth and pulled forwards with both hands, hearing the rip of more damaged fabric.

"I hate you! Get out of my life!" She swung the trousers up towards her bedroom ceiling and slammed them down, then jumped on the pile of crumpled blue on her bedroom floor.

In a sudden, unearthly breeze, the trousers whipped up and wrapped around her neck. Angela pulled as hard as she could, but with each tug, they tightened like a boa constrictor, throttling her throat.

"Help! Stephen…"

White pinpricks of light danced before her and she saw the veins inside her eyeballs as they bulged. The air left her lungs. Her legs began to sink, folding beneath her and darkness consumed.

***

"I hate you. Get out of my life!"

Violet pointed towards the front door of her flat. Jamel put up both hands and shook his head.

"Damn, V, what is with you lately? Your mood swings change quicker than the weather. It's not like you."

Violet snatched her aromatherapy burner off the glass coffee table and hurled it at him. He ducked and sidestepped to the left, bringing his right arm up in a parry to deflect it, and it cracked against the wall, splintering into thousands of pieces.

"Don't think your boxing is going to save you from what I'll do to you, you cheating bastard. How could you – with my best friend – on Valentine's Day."

Jamel's eyes, full of innocent confusion, widened. "I never have – and never would – be unfaithful to you."

"I saw you coming out of her house, don't lie. Why would you be there without me?"

"You followed me?" His face was full of hurt.

"Yes, and I'm glad I did. What reason would you have to be at Sandra's place other than to fuck her. I've seen how she looks at you, how she always flirts with you."

He took a few steps towards her, reaching out with soothing hands. "You've got this all wrong."

"Liar." Violet ducked under his arm and grabbed her coffee mug off the table. Before he could react, she swung it against his head.

It was as if the scene that followed happened in slow motion; the mug struck him in the middle of his forehead and splintered in a shower of ceramic, causing blood to splatter over his face. Jamel staggered and tripped on her living room rug, falling backwards. As he arced towards the floor, she watched with horror as his head cracked against the tiled fireplace and he lay with his eyes glassy and wide, a trickle of blood running from the corner of his open mouth to match the splatter on his forehead wound.

"Oh my God, what have I done?" Violet clapped both hands over her nose and mouth, breathing in her recycled air to steady herself as she walked backwards. Her head felt light and her legs weak.

"Jamel, baby, I'm so sorry. It was an accident. I – I wasn't thinking straight. I'm so sorry. Forgive me."

She snapped to her senses and raced to his side. First to check his pulse. Nothing. Now his neck. Still nothing.

How to do CPR? Think. Think. She had never learned. Instead, she pummelled on his chest and breathed hopeless gasps of air into his mouth.

"Please – Jamel – don't be dead. I'm sorry."

The neckline of her top tightened on her throat as the fabric snaked down her back, catching on her blue velvet trousers while she bent over her dead lover. Violet hooked her fingers inside the neckline and tugged, trying to detach it from her throat. It pulled so tight she began to gag. The velvet trousers seemed to pull as though the trousers had a life of their own, pulling like unseen hands at the base of her back.

As she writhed, her knee nudged Jamel's dead body and a small box tumbled out of his pocket. A ring box. The truth struck her; he had been hiding an engagement ring. He wasn't cheating with Sandra; on the contrary, her best friend had been helping Jamel to plan a secret proposal that they both wanted to surprise Violet with.

Remorseful tears welled in her eyes.

"Help! I'm sorry," she croaked. "Jamel, help."

The trousers pulled so low, tugging the back of her top until it cut into her neck. Tearing threads sounded in her ears. Was she going to be strangled to death by her favourite blue velvet trousers, a Valentine's Day present from the man she loved – and had killed?

Like a tug of war, the hem of Violet's top broke free from the grip of her trousers. She fell back, clutching at her neck and gasping mouthfuls of precious, life-giving air, filling her lungs.

In a sudden flurry, the blue velvet trousers hurled down her legs and whipped off her feet. They looped up over Violet's body and wrapped themselves around her neck, once, twice, three times, tight as a scarf. After they had secured themselves in place around her neck they began to choke her. Tighter. Tighter. She watched her reflection in the glassy coffee table as her face turned red, then violet, matching her name, before finally turning blue.

I'm sorry. I don't want to die. I want to spend my life with you, Jamel.

But the words couldn't escape her mouth. Nothing escaped her mouth as death closed in on her, silent and strong.

As Violet lay dying on her living room floor, the blue velvet trousers released their vice-like grip on her neck and lay, quiet and benign in between the lovers.

***

"Bloody hell, Angela. What's going on?"

Fingers. Fingers hooking themselves between the trousers and her neck, creating a gap. A gap that allowed her to breath. A lifesaving gap.

"Stephen," she gasped. "I called for you, and you came."

He ripped the trousers off her throat and hurled them across the room. "The weirdest thing happened. I was watching the football, and then the TV flickered. It went all static, you know, and then this blonde woman appeared on the screen. She was wearing trousers like those–"

Angela glanced sideways at the blue, velvet trousers.

"Then the next minute, she appeared in my living room, but she was see-through like a ghost. She beckoned to me to follow her, and I suddenly heard you calling to me." He massaged his eyes with a thumb and forefinger. "All I could think of was getting over to your house because I somehow knew you were in trouble, so I jumped in the car."

"The trousers tried to strangle me. They were possessed. It's too weird to explain, but I'll try. The girl you saw was called Violet. Her boyfriend Jamel bought them for her last year for Valentine's Day. They were a passionate couple, but jealous too. She killed him in an accident, and then the trousers killed her. I think all their pent-up passion and rage somehow went into the trousers and caused them to become possessed."

Stephen blinked at her. "You're saying, the ghosts of Violet and Jamel are inside the trousers?"

"Or their energy, their life-force, from when they were alive," she added.

He sat back on his haunches. "That would explain a lot."

She noticed a blush form across his cheeks and the bridge of his nose and understood.

Heat formed in her ears and the back of her neck; the sex had been *wild*. "You mean – what happened between us?"

He cast a sheepish grin at her. "Ahem – if what you say is true, that the trousers are possessed, then I think you should take them back to the shop where you got them."

"I tried that, but they reappeared here." She pointed at her bed.

He looked at the spot on her bed where she indicated and stroked his chin, thinking. "In that case, maybe you should burn them That would surely release the energy, or ghosts, or whatever you want to call them?"

Angela jumped to her feet. "Great idea."

She snatched the trousers in one hand and hurried downstairs, Stephen following close behind. As she reached the hallway, she saw the broken glass of the window next to the door. Stephen cared so much, he had broken his way into her house to save her. Her chest swelled with affection for him. Unlike her previous lust, this time she felt her feelings were real.

Despite the chill February air, she led them into her back garden, still wearing only her red jumper and knickers. Stephen grabbed a bottle of vodka from her kitchen counter and Angela dumped the trousers on the grass, letting him pour the alcohol over them.

"Have you got a lighter?" He raised his eyebrows.

"There's a clicker in the second kitchen drawer," she said, feeling warmth at his resourcefulness. Who could resist such a sexy man who could take charge?

Stephen returned with the safety lighter and lit the vodka-soaked trousers.

As the flames licked high into the cold winter twilight, two flickering lights danced out of the fire. One was a beautiful, slim, blonde-haired woman and the other a handsome, dark-skinned man. The couple weaved as smoke coils around each other and as the circles widened, enclosing Angela and Stephen, they spoke to them.

"Thank you," said Violet.

"You've saved us," Jamel added.

"Be free together in heaven," Angela replied.

Her eyes were still on the floating couple, spinning around them, when she felt warm fingers slip in between hers and a firm grip on her hand. She turned her face towards Stephen and saw him smiling at her.

It had been a weird-o-rama week for sure, so what did she have to lose? Only one way to find out if the passion between them was real or caused by the trousers. Angela leaned in for a kiss. His hand slipped around behind her waist, pulling her closer.

"Better late than never, but Happy belated Valentine's Day," he said, before their lips met and the smoke whirled around them.

"I love you, Jamel," said Angela.

Stephen's blue eyes turned dark for a moment, before he answered. "I love you too, Violet."

4

Cassandra's Call

Another year. Alone.

Patrick listened to the creak of the floorboards in the flat above his. He could hear every laugh, every voice singing along to a host of noughties favourites as they had yet another party. Did all youngsters listen to oldies these days; was no decent music produced any more?

Not that he was much older than them, at thirty-three. In fact, he was a 'young' thirty-something; one that could easily pass for twenty-three or twenty-four. If he were to sidle upstairs and slip into the party, he was sure no one would notice that he wasn't yet another student.

His mind was made up. He would go to their Valentine's Day party and hopefully meet someone nice.

Patrick pulled on a t-shirt and cargo trousers, the most hip and trendy thing he owned; and made a note not to use the words 'hip' or 'trendy' with the Gen Z lot upstairs. What lingo did kids use currently, anyway?

Not that it would matter. They would surely all be too sloshed to notice, or care what he said anyway.

He wound his way up the two concrete flights on the stairwell and was happy to see that the front door of party central was open, and heaving with young lads and lasses, mingling with their plastic cups of who-knew-what. He brushed aside his feelings of being the old man at the party, and slipped in between the hot, heavy throng.

What a relief that nobody seemed to take any notice of him. He squeezed through the masses towards the kitchen; the layout was exactly the same as his flat below, so he found it quickly. A drink of whatever was on offer for Dutch courage was the plan, and he would see if there was anyone interesting looking to talk to. It made a change from the numerous dating apps that had resulted in a few cringeworthy dates, never to be repeated.

He saw her as soon as he turned into the kitchen and the sight of her stopped him in his tracks, and made his breath catch in his chest. She had long black hair that was so dark, it had a bluish reflection in the bare kitchen lightbulb. It hung to her slim waist. She had a short fringe that dusted her forehead in a perfectly straight line. Her eyes were green like emeralds, and round, like those of a porcelain doll. Her dark eyebrows arched over them, giving her a mournful expression, even when she smiled, showing two rows of even white teeth. Her skin was smooth and creamy, with no tinge of a blush even over her high cheekbones. She was strikingly beautiful. Engrossed in conversation with a nondescript blonde-haired friend, she didn't notice him at all.

The mysterious brunette beauty stood with her back to the sink as she talked. Her right arm was strapped across her stomach, cradling her left elbow, and she held a plastic cup with a red drink in it; probably wine or port. Patrick couldn't help but note how similarly dressed to him she was, with her khaki-coloured cargo trousers. She also wore a form-fitting white t-shirt that cut above her stomach, showing her belly button.

She was by far the most attractive person in the whole party. Amazing that none of the other blokes there had made a move by now, considering the Valentine's Day party had been going for a couple of hours, at least. Now was his chance. He simply had to talk to her.

Patrick squeezed through the crowded kitchen and reached for a stack of plastic cups.

"Excuse me," he said to the mysterious beauty. "I just want to get a glass of water."

She turned her round, green eyes to him. "Cup."

"Pardon?" he said. The loud music made it hard to heard what she said, but it sounded like 'yup'.

She pointed to his plastic cup. "It isn't a glass, it's a cup."

"Oh, er, right." He looked at the cup in his hands, feeling a flush of heat spread over his face.

The awkwardness in their exchange clearly made the woman's companion uncomfortable; the blonde friend turned her back on them and began a conversation with a nearby man.

Patrick gathered himself; wasn't it a bit rude of her, in fact, to correct a perfect stranger like that? Rude or not, he still felt like a schoolboy in her presence.

The girl laughed a soft, tinkling sound that put him at ease. "Sorry to be a pedant, I was just joshing with you. I'm an English major."

Only a joke; he needed to lighten up. Patrick allowed himself to relax and laughed with her.

"Wouldn't you rather have some wine? Or do you not drink?"

Again, he felt like a schoolboy being subjected to peer-pressure. He swallowed, reminding himself of his age. "Um, sure. I'll have whatever you're having."

She poured him a large glass of red wine. He sipped, resisting the urge to wince. Red wine always gave him heartburn, and the liquid was very tart. The woman smiled at him over the top of her own glass. Patrick gulped more of the dry wine. Dutch courage, that was all that mattered. This beautiful woman was out of his league, but all her attention was on him. If he had even an inkling of a chance with her, it was worth the stomachache.

"What's your name?" she asked, in a voice as smooth as silk.

Patrick tried to speak, but his tongue felt heavy. Why was the woman so intoxicating that he was getting tongue-tied like an awkward adolescent with his first crush?

"Let me see. Hmm." She winced with concentration, her nose wrinkling in an adorable manner. "It's Paddy, isn't it?"

Patrick recoiled. "How did you know?"

"You *look* like a Patrick." One corner of her mouth twitched upwards.

Best to go with her flirtatious lead. "My turn to guess your name. Hmm. I'm going to go with Jessica."

More tinkling laughter from her, this time with her head thrown back. "Not quite. I'm Cassandra. But my friends call me Sandy."

He grinned. "Does that mean I'm a friend?"

She let her sexy smile fade and fixed him with a look of – of what? Was there a hint of lust in those mysterious, green eyes?

"Maybe," she teased.

He dared to move closer. "Or maybe more?"

"Mmm. Perhaps."

He sidled even closer. She had a dusting of tiny freckles on the bridge of her nose.

"I prefer Cassandra. It's a beautiful name. Unusual."

She lifted her chin, ever so slowly, until their eyes met. Her lips were slightly parted and her chest rose and fell with small breaths. They were so close, their fingers almost touched. His face was mere inches from hers; if he lowered his head now, he could easily kiss her. The energy between them was electric, the moment intimate, even though they didn't touch. Just held each other's gazes, in time and space, and the crowd around them, the flat, the whole building – melted away.

***

What a brilliant party. It had given him a chance to meet such an amazing girl. An incredible girl. The perfect girl for him. She was intelligent, studying English, with a desire to become a teacher. Not only that, but stunning too. Valentine's Day had ended with a kiss. Her lips had been soft, and her kiss light, but passionate. There had been a taste of salt in her mouth, just a touch. Her hair had smelled of fruit shampoo. He had walked her out to her taxi, then climbed the stairs back to his flat, feeling over the moon.

Patrick flopped back on his bed, his heart lighter than air, as his head swirled with thoughts of Cassandra. Was it too soon to text her? No harm in sending just a quick follow-up to make sure she got home safely, wherever home was.

Hope u got home safely. Would be lovely to c u again sometime. Paddy :)

Send. Now what? That wasn't too forward of him, was it? He didn't care of the etiquette; if he wanted a date, he'd have to be direct.

A strip of light showing under his bedroom door roused Patrick and he sat up. The landing light had switched on. What on earth? He watched with horror as the door handle began to turn, the round brass knob rotating.

Patrick jumped out of bed and grabbed the nearest weapon he could find; the bedside lamp. He brandished it by the base, ready to swing it like a baseball bat. If it was a burglar, they would be very sorry for breaking into his flat.

Anger turned to disbelief as a shock of long, black hair appeared around the side of the door, followed by a long, lithe leg. Cassandra slid into the room. She was wearing a short, white satin dress with spaghetti straps;

a sexy nightdress. One leg laced over the top of the other, in a catwalk gait, as she glided over to his bed.

It had to be a dream. Patrick felt as though he had lost the ability to blink as he watched her, unwilling to miss even a moment of her beauty before him.

Cassandra slid one spaghetti strap off her shoulder and then the other, letting her dress drop to below her small, pert breasts. His eyes flicked to her pale, pink nipples before darting back up to her face. She continued the tease, tugging the dress on downwards until it dropped to the floor, and she stood, naked, at the foot of his bed.

"You said it would be lovely to see me again sometime," she said, in her soft, feminine voice.

His heart hammered. "This has got to be a dream. I only texted that a few minutes ago."

She bent one leg and rested her knee on his bed, then climbed onto the mattress.

He looked up at her, as she crawled on all fours towards him, her long, black hair dangling forwards and casting her face into shadow. Cassandra kneeled over him, with one leg on either side of his hips. With her legs parted, he could see all of her bare form exposed in the soft glow from the landing light.

"You aren't really here. I must be dreaming," he continued, his breath barely more than a whisper.

"I'm as real as you want me to be." She looked down at him, her lips parted in a soft smile.

That confirmed it; he was dreaming. A great dream. The best.

Patrick put his hand on the top of her warm left thigh and slid it upwards, moving to the inside of her thigh. Cassandra didn't move, allowing his hand to explore upwards. Did he dare venture more? She hadn't stopped him, clearly wanting him to. He moved his hand into the warmth of her dark pubic area and pushed one finger inside. There was resistance from her body, which felt tight. The sensation excited him; he explored with another. A slight tug on his fingers surprised him, as though her body pulled from the inside. He pumped his fingers in and out, feeling her wetness, but each time the pull from within was stronger; almost like a suction. A warm damp spread over his whole hand and wrist. Was she that excited? It took him a moment to realise that it wasn't fluid from her body running out; his hand had been pulled inside her.

Followed by his arm up to his elbow.

Followed by the whole length up to his shoulder.

Warm darkness shrouded him; the landing light had either been extinguished or blocked from view. What was happening? All around felt cushiony and wet. There was a faint earthy smell; not unpleasant, just like that of wet soil. He reached out and felt a soft, powdery substance like fine clay, or sand. Even with his eyes wide open, he couldn't see anything.

"Cassandra?"

What a strange dream. Why couldn't there have been more of the erotic part and less of the being swallowed inside her vagina part. Where was he? A ravine? Wherever he was, he knew he was alone.

"Hello?"

He could see a line of light far above, out of reach. The smell of damp sand was strong. It reminded him of a time he had been hiking in the Jurassic Coast in Devon, on Valentine's Day, a decade before. The light grew brighter until it consumed him and as he adjusted, he saw that he was back in his bedroom with the landing light casting a glow across his bedroom.

A dream. A strange dream. Wasn't it?

But it had been so vivid.

The smell of the Jurassic Coast lingered in his nostrils. Such a sensation after waking from a dream, had never happened before. The memory of that hiking excursion was vivid. He had been visiting his younger brother, Marcus, who was in his first year studying Earth Sciences at Exeter. Marcus had a date lined up on Valentine's Day with his dream girl, Janey, from his course and had begged Patrick to come along on a double date; Janey's condition for agreeing to a date in the first place. Her friend had been socially awkward and difficult to talk to; Patrick recalled trying to make polite conversation with the girl as they had weaved along the coastal path. Along the trail, his date had disappeared. He assumed she had got bored at their awkward small talk and had most likely gone home. Concerned, he had caught up with Marcus and Janey, who were further ahead, and asked them to text the girl. Turned out she had gone home, as he suspected.

What a blow to his ego. He had been emasculated by a date that *he* had found boring, not the other way round. Boring and hard to talk to; and apparently she had thought the same of him. On the other hand, the date had ended well for Marcus; his Valentine's Day date, Janey, was now his wife.

Patrick had spent the decade since that awkward double date feeling like a loser with women. If even a socially awkward girl – whose name he couldn't even recall – had stood him up in the middle of a hiking trail date, then what hope did he have with women he *actually* wanted to date?

Until now, of course.

In spite of the weird, provocative – and frankly bizarre – dream about Cassandra, he couldn't wait to see her again. She was a perfect ten in every way: interesting, fascinating, and stunning. A real catch.

***

Patrick sat outside on his lunch break, enjoying a rare sunny day for mid-February. He took a bite out of his chicken baguette and scrolled through his phone feed with the other hand.

"Hello."

The breathy voice in his ear and warm lips brushing against his cheek made his heart hammer. Cassandra stood behind him with a wide grin. She wore a tight-fitting black t-shirt that showed her toned stomach and mint-green cargo trousers. An image of dream-Cassandra, wearing a white satin nightdress floated in his mind. He blinked to dismiss it, worried that such a thought might make him blush.

"Cassandra. Fancy seeing you here."

"I'm on my way to a lecture."

In the commercial district? Why would she be cutting through the business park where he worked? The university was on the other side of the city centre; he didn't speak his thoughts though. Seeing her was a breath of fresh air from his IT colleagues.

"Well, good timing for me then. I'm on my lunch break."

Her eyes rested on his phone. "Really? I was sure you were working out here."

He opened his mouth to explain, before realising she was joking.

"You have quite the sardonic sense of humour," he guffawed. "Always keeping me on my toes."

She chortled with her tinkling laughter. "I know you love it really."

Gawd, she was smoking hot. An irresistible urge to kiss her seized him and Patrick bounced up onto the balls of his feet. Cassandra didn't seem surprised in the slightest; in fact, she leaned her face forward to meet his. He closed his eyes and leaned in to kiss her.

As their lips met, the familiar pull that he recognised from his dream tugged his face forward. The salty taste on her plump lips grew stronger as she opened her mouth. Warm wetness spread over his cheeks and upwards over the bridge of his nose. Curious, Patrick opened his eyes.

It was as though he was falling into a terracotta-coloured cave. Warm, spongy dampness enclosed him from the walls of the cave. Creamy stalactites dangled down from above, while thick stalagmites jutted upwards. Behind, the daylight grew narrower and narrower as darkness began to consume him.

What was happening? This was *no* dream?

A terrified shriek rumbled out of Patrick's throat and echoed in the spongy cavern. He tripped over the stalagmites as he fought his way towards the light and tumbled forward out of the cave in a flood of warm, sticky water.

"What on earth? What just happened?" He gasped, his chest heaving. Patrick scooted backwards like a crab as Cassandra reappeared before him, wiping saliva off her chin and fixing her smile back in place.

"I thought you wanted to taste me. I wanted to taste you too," she purred.

"What? What's going on?" He stumbled to his feet and backed away from her. His head was spinning.

It wasn't a dream. Whatever was going on wasn't a dream.

"Didn't you like to be inside me?" She pointed to her mouth.

The cave. The terracotta cave. It wasn't a cave. It was her gaping maw.

"What the fuck are you?" he screamed.

"I'm the woman you've been missing all these years," she said, with a sweet smile. "Your dream girl."

"You aren't a girl or a woman." He pointed a shaking finger at her. "What are you? What do you want with me?"

Her smile faded. "Don't you know? Don't you remember?"

She took a step towards him, her smile now completely gone. In the absence of her stunning grin, her expression was blank. Without her smile, her face looked different.

What had changed about her? Patrick was so curious, he stopped backing away from her and looked closer, studying her. The dusting of freckles across her nose spread until there were freckles all over her face. Her large, round green eyes grew smaller. Her arched, doll-like eyebrows became straight lines. Her creamy complexion became pale, with dark circles under her eyes. Her straight, glossy black hair became dull with a slight frizz at the crown.

"You. I recognise you–" He pointed a shaking finger at her. The Valentine's Day double date, a decade before. Janey's friend.

"Now you remember me. Now you know my name – Cassandra."

He felt sick. "But how? You're back to how you looked a decade ago. You haven't aged."

She threw her head back, full of tinkling laughter. "Isn't that a mystery?"

He shook his head. "No, this isn't possible. If I'm not dreaming, then I must be going mad. Where's Cassandra – the other one who was just here? The one I met a few days ago on Valentine's Day?"

The woman standing before him changed again, the contours of her face melting and blending until the beautiful, doll-like Cassandra that he knew from his neighbours' party stood before him.

"Is that better?" she teased.

Patrick trembled from head to toe.

"Want to know how I did this?"

He wanted to say no, but he was shaking too much. He felt completely unable to control his body. Cassandra stepped closer, closer and opened her mouth. Her jaw dropped low and kept lengthening and widening until her gaping maw became the terracotta cave that had engulfed him when they kissed. Now it was all consuming.

Patrick was lifted off his feet and felt himself falling forwards inside the cavern of her throat. Downwards he fell, head over heels, into darkness. At what felt like an eternity later, he landed on a slimy, spongy surface that pulsated with a steady rhythm.

Ba-boom. Ba-boom.

An image began to form in the darkness. It was as though he was watching a movie on a screen projected before him. A student bedroom appeared, with a planner on the wall and a desk with pens and folders.

A black-haired girl perched on the bed. She cuddled a red, heart-shaped cushion to her chest. Patrick recognised the girl from his Valentine's Day double date ten years before.

"Whatever god is listening to me right now, hear my prayer. All I want is for my blind date today to be my soulmate. Let our souls join as one. I'm tired of being plain Cassandra, boring Cassandra. Sexy Janey's friend. Let this man today notice me, want me, desire me. Let no other woman compare to me. For that, I'll do anything. I'll worship you every day if you'll only grant me this one wish."

The bedroom scene faded and a new projection formed; he saw himself, at twenty-three years of age, hiking along the Jurassic Coast with Marcus, Janey and her friend.

"Patrick, this is Sandy. Sandy, meet Patrick."

He watched his younger self shaking hands with the girl. His date offered a shy smile, averting her eyes. Younger Patrick's eyes were on the clifftop scenery more than his date. The two young couples set off along the cliff-side path and he listened to the awkward small-talk he had made with the girl.

But, how had she transformed into the beautiful siren that had swallowed him whole?

He kept watching. The distance between his younger self, in the projected memory, and Sandy grew as he powered ahead, leaving her trailing behind on the coastal cliff path. She huffed, and puffed, red in the face from the effort to keep up.

"Wait for me! I can't keep up with you outdoorsy types."

Sandy, the English major, who wanted to be a teacher. The suave, sexy Cassandra at his neighbour's

Valentine's Day party a few days earlier had revealed that much.

Sandy panted along, falling further behind.

Her foot stepped too close to the edge.

Down. Sliding down, tumbling down, her shriek of surprise muffled by the wind and the distance between them.

Onto the rocks, Sandy's body was broken.

Into the sea, consumed by death.

Out of the waves, given new life.

Patrick watched agape as stunning Cassandra, brand new Cassandra, emerged from the water. Her hair was perfectly sleek. Her skin was perfectly smooth. Her green eyes were wide, and bright, and round. Cassandra was reborn as Satan's servant.

"Quite the upgrade, isn't it?" Cassandra's omnipotent voice echoed in the dark cavern of her chest, where he resided.

"I lost my confidence with women because of you. I thought you stood me up that day, when all along you had sold your soul to the Devil."

"I did it all for you. Don't you see? You're the privileged one. You're my chosen one. My soulmate," her voice echoed.

He shook his head in the darkness. "I'm not your soulmate. I don't do deals with Satan."

"It's too late for that. All these years, I called to you. My calls kept you submissive. They kept you down. They kept other women away. You were too insecure for dating. Your relationships never worked out. Don't you see? That was me, all along, calling to you. Until eventually, the time was right. You were desperate enough to be ready for our souls to become one."

"You're mad," he shouted. "Let me out of here. I'll never love you. You've got my body trapped, but you can't take my mind."

Laughter. Vicious, cold-blooded laughter rattled through the chamber of her chest. Patrick staggered with the vibrations and fell to his knees.

"You'll learn to love me in time. Like me, you're now immortal. You're inside of me, you're part of me.

"I'll never love you."

"I called to you, and you came. That means your mind already belongs to me. Your eternal soul now belongs to me too. I swallowed your body, so I have all of you, my forever Valentine."

With that, the echoes of his own terrified screams deafened his ears as Patrick sank into the black oblivion, deep in the abyss of Cassandra's lost soul.

5

A Haunted Lupercalia

Maisie staggered into her hallway and dropped her keys. Her head was swimming with too much wine. It had been a necessity for the speed dating night, but that last bloke – what was his name? – Kyle? Yeah, that or Keith. Keith or Kyle had been sort of interesting. Maybe enough for a second date. What was it he said he did? He tested smoke alarm installations. Could come in handy. One time when she'd had a few too many, she had fallen asleep with a fag in her hand. Luckily it had snuffed out on the quilt leaving only a charred hole, though she shivered at the memory; it could've been so much worse.

She kicked off her silver stilettos and enjoyed the cool massage of the tiles on her swollen feet. The things she did to attract the opposite sex. Granted, it was Valentine's Day. Dressing up in her favourite slutty dress and porn star heels was worth it, if it bagged her a second date.

What was his name? Kevin?

Kyle. No, Keith.

Ah, sod it. Her alcohol-soaked brain could sort out the whole name-business in the morning.

"Mylo? Mylo, baby, where are you? Mummy is waiting."

Maisie checked the living room. No sign of her miniature schnauzer in her bed by the radiator. Kitchen next. He was probably having a snack.

Highly unusual that he wasn't there either. Hmm. Where could he have gone?

"Mylo? Come here, baby. Mummy is starting to get worried."

She turned to the dog flap. Mylo never went out at night. Or was that only because he was usually tucked up at the foot of her bed? Had her rare date-night out thrown him out of whack, and he had decided to go for a late night excursion too, maybe even to look for her?

Maisie slipped on her muddy trainers and duffel coat over her short, sequinned dress, and ventured out into the lamplit street. She glanced at her phone. Quarter past twelve. Thank goodness there weren't many cars about. Mylo was white, which would reflect well in car headlights, but he was small. A car might squash him flat before he had a chance to escape.

She cupped her mouth with her hands, making her voice echo in the thick air. "Mylo!"

A shroud of fog lingering around the lamppost lights gave the pre-dawn hours an eerie, otherworldly feel. She rubbed her arms, then her hands together and kept going. Where had that rascal got to?

There were no lights on in any of her neighbours' houses. Maisie kept walking, weaving her way through the cul-de-sacs of new build houses until the edge of the development. There, a small wood separated the residential area from a large field, the size of a football stadium, where archaeologists worked during the day. Old Harry, down in the post office, said they had found the remains of a Roman cemetery dating back more than two thousand years.

Mylo wouldn't have gone into the woods, or onto the archaeological excavation, would he?

"My-lo? My-lo! There's a good boy."

She swallowed her fears. He was twelve years old, nearing thirteen. He couldn't run as fast as he used to, and wasn't used to being far from home; definitely not at night. What if–?

No. It didn't bear thinking about. She would find him, and bring him home safely.

Maisie veered left into the dark woods. During the day, she appreciated a small patch of nature so close to her house, but now at night, the dense, black patch of trees seemed spooky. She blew warm air into her hands, rubbed them together against the chill, and set off into the woods.

Was it her imagination or did the fog seem to swirl behind her, enclosing her within the trees? As she cast a glance over her shoulder, she had half a mind to turn back and go to her warm bed. The effects of the copious wine she had consumed on her speed date had worn off; now she had only adrenaline and fear.

No; she had to be strong. Be strong for Mylo. Her poor baby was somewhere out in the darkness, probably more terrified than she was.

"Mummy's coming, Mylo."

She pushed through the trees on the other side and found herself at the makeshift fence the archaeologists had erected. There was a gap between the metal barrier, enough for her arm all the way up to the shoulder. She pried the fencing apart, widening it until she could squeeze through sideways.

At least the moonlight showed the field more clearly than the dark woods, where no light could penetrate. The fog didn't seem to be lingering either; the clear view bolstered her confidence.

Still, she needed to keep her wits about her. It looked like the excavation team had dug holes all over the place. There were circular ones the size of dinner plates and rectangular ones that could have fit a microwave inside. A large rectangular one drew her eye; her feet followed towards it, her old trainers squelching on the soft, muddy ground.

Was it a grave? She couldn't say why it attracted her attention. She paced nearer, nearer, and peered over the edge.

"No. Oh my God, Mylo, no!"

Her little white schnauzer, her companion, lay inside a shallow pit of half a metre deep. He lay on his side, as if he was sleeping, on top of old, scattered bones. His chest wasn't rising and falling.

Maisie jumped down into the rectangular pit and grabbed her dog. "Mylo, wake up. It's okay, mummy is here. Mylo?"

She held him to her chest.

"Mylo?"

Her voice was high pitched and verging on hysteria in the silence.

"Mylo!"

"Are you alright?"

Maisie screamed and spun around. She held Mylo's limp body in one arm and clapped her hand against her chest with the other.

A man peered over the edge of the pit. She could see him well, outlined by the moonlight as if he glowed. He had dark hair that curled across his forehead and long, angular eyes, with straight, serious eyebrows. His clothing struck her as unusual; he wore a long garment that looked like a toga in a light colour; maybe white or cream. Even the sight of him wearing such little clothing in the chill February air made her shiver.

"It's my dog." She held Mylo out in her extended arms.

The man looked down at her pet. "It seems he came here and passed on. Was he aged?"

She nodded, unable to speak, and fought against the prickle forming in the corners of her eyes.

"He had a long and happy life with you. You should feel reassured that he passed on in no pain, in comfort," he soothed.

"How could you possibly know that? He died out here in the cold, alone, and not at home in my arms, in our warm bed," she sobbed.

Maisie curled over the small body of her dog and cried, her tears wetting his soft, white fur.

"There, there," he said, in a soft, but affirmative voice. His deep, soothing, baritone manner made her look up and she sniffed away tears to find him standing beside her in the pit.

"Why are you dressed like that?"

"A party. Sometimes we have to wear what is expected of us. This was the required dress code."

Must have been a toga party; although the guy looked older than a student. She would have put him at, what? Late twenties? Early thirties?

Up close, the man was really quite handsome. Maisie felt a tug in her stomach, deep down in her gut, churning up her insides. Her intestines were practically somersaulting into a heart-shaped knot. He had a Latin look about him, a kind of Mediterranean appeal. Who was that old time movie star he reminded her of? Rudolph Valentino?

Blimey, the bloke was *on fire*.

"I'd like to help you, if you'll let me," he said.

"Thank you. I need to get him home. I want to put him in his bed, one last time," she sniffed.

She set Mylo at the side of the pit and climbed out side by side with the man, then scooped her dog up into her arms.

"I can accompany you home, to see that you get there safely," he suggested.

"I'd appreciate that. I don't even know you, but I know that I don't want to be alone. I hope it isn't too much bother?"

"None at all," he reassured.

"I don't live far from here – just in the new build homes on the other side of the woods. Do you live nearby?"

"I'm from around here," he said, his face fixed ahead.

She couldn't help but glance at his toned arms and shoulders, and his taut physique that was exposed above his toga. "Aren't you cold in that thing? I'm freezing and I've got a coat on."

"I'm used to the cold," he quipped, with a smile.

They passed through the woods, the heavy fog swirling on the outskirts, and weaved through the streets towards her house. As they reached her doorstep, the heavy fog was a blanket around them, obscuring the moon.

"Thanks for walking me home. Do you want to come in and get warmed up for a minute?"

The words had barely left her mouth and regret set in. She didn't want him to get the wrong impression.

"I mean, for a hot cocoa or something?" she added.

He smiled. "That would be nice."

Her forehead tightened; again with the regret. Hadn't she just invited a perfect stranger into her house? I mean, what if he turned out to be an axe murderer?

Instead, the strange man took off his sandals at her front door and entered in his bare feet. "Do you have a basin of water? I would like to wash my feet before I join you for a drink."

What an unusual gentleman. She *liked* it. She *really* liked it. It was an eccentric suggestion, a custom she'd never heard of. But it seemed chivalrous, and respectful. There was no way this guy was a murderer. She felt safe with him.

"Well, the bathroom is right upstairs, if you like?" She pointed up the carpeted stairs, which were opposite the front door, separating the living room from the kitchen; a quirky layout in her newly built house.

The toga-clad man stepped off the tiled floor by the entrance and looked down at the fluffy, beige carpet. He curled his toes, gripping the fabric, then let out a chuckle of surprise.

"What manner of – stuff – is this?"

For a split second, she thought he was referring to dirt stuck on the bare soles of his feet, but then noticed him grabbing the carpet with his toes. "Um, are you talking about my carpet?"

He hopped up and down, giddy in a manner that belied his age. "What kind of sheep did you shear to get this? The legendary golden fleece?"

Maisie let out a nervous chuckle. "Erm, it's just polyester, I think. Listen, why don't you get washed upstairs and I'll just put Mylo in his pet bed until the morning."

The man disappeared upstairs as she busied herself in the kitchen, laying the body of her beloved pet to rest in his bed for one final time. A few minutes later, he appeared in the doorway as she left the kitchen. For the first time since she had arrived home, a chill swept over her, raising goosebumps across her back and shoulders. Time to crank up the heating, perhaps.

"Can I get you a hot drink, em – sorry, I didn't catch your name?"

"Amatus," he said, the corners of his mouth dimpling in a sexy smile.

"Amatus? I've never heard that before. I like that." She rubbed her clammy palms against the sides of her thighs to compose herself. "I'm Maisie."

"Maisie." He mouthed her name with a thoughtfulness as though he was testing the syllables; trying out the sound of her name on his tongue. "May-see. Where does that come from, Maisie?"

"Erm, I think it's Scottish. My family are originally from the Highlands, though we've lived in England for generations." She shook her hands in an apologetic gesture. "What would you like to drink?"

His eyebrows dipped upwards in a pensive manner. "I wouldn't say no to a glass of some quality Conditum, if you have any."

Maisie's brain came to a standstill. "Uh, sorry, what?"

"It's fine if you don't have any. Maybe you Pictish folk up north don't have any Conditum? You add a touch of honey to the wine, and a dash of pepper with some seawater if there's any going."

"Pardon?" She could feel one of her eyebrows practically hitting the roof. "Wine with what?"

"Conditum?" One of Amatus' eyebrows seemed to have hit the roof in response. "But a cup of Lora will do fine, if that's all you have."

Conditum? Lora? She had never heard of those brands of wine. From the tone of his voice, he was suggesting moderately expensive wines, and wondering if he needed to lower the threshold. "I was thinking more along the lines of hot cocoa, but if it's wine you're after, there's half a bottle of chardonnay in the fridge?"

"That would be lovely," he said.

Maisie crossed the kitchen and opened the fridge. Amatus recoiled with a gasp. He pointed a shaking finger at her. "By Jove, what is that?"

She glanced at the bottle of chardonnay in her hand and back to his startled face. "What, this? It's the only wine I have, I'm afraid."

"Not that. What manner of sorcery is that metal contraption of yours? It's putting out cold air."

She looked at the fridge. Was he for real?

She looked back at Amatus. "A-ha. I think I follow. You're doing some kind of role-play. You're playing the part of a Roman. Is this an acting gig? Is that why you're wearing the toga?"

Amatus' face was blank. "I'm sorry, I don't follow."

As she shut the fridge, closing out the bright glow from within, a shadow passed across Amatus' face. It cloaked his handsome face and instead showed a new impression; the bony outline of a skull and dark, hollow orbital sockets in place of his chiselled features.

Maisie screamed and clapped her hands over her face, enclosing her mouth and nose. She staggered backwards until she bumped against the fridge.

"What's going on? What *are* you?"

As her eyes adjusted to the dim kitchen light bulb, his normal features resumed, but a chill lingered along her spine.

"You can't be a hallucination. I didn't drink that much alcohol tonight."

His eyes, and his mouth made perfect circles of surprise. "What do you mean *what am I?* Hallucination, you say?"

"Well, it's just that I think my eyes must be playing tricks on me. Just now you looked like a skeleton," she gasped.

He gave a solemn nod. "Ah, I see. That makes sense. Then it's true."

What was true? A feeling of deep dread settled in the pit of her stomach. She didn't want her gut feeling to be right. It couldn't possibly be right; could it?

"You're a ghost, aren't you?" she choked out.

He nodded. "I suspected as much. I started to wonder why things had changed so much, yet I hadn't. The town where I lived gradually fell to ruins as the people moved on. Strangers came wearing equally strange clothing, and speaking an odd tongue that I didn't recognise. Sometimes it seemed as if I was asleep for a time, and when I returned, life had moved on from me in confusing ways. I began to get lonely. I had no friends, no family, and when I tried to talk to people, they either ignored me, or would shiver and walk away. The language changed, many times. It took me a while to learn this guttural language that you speak, but I picked it up. I had nothing else to do but observe."

Maisie hesitated. She had so much to ask. Her curiosity was too strong. "Do you remember how you, you know, how did you pass on?"

"You mean, how I died?" His eyes became unfocused at a point behind her. "I can't say for sure. I recall feeling a sharp pain between my shoulder blades, followed by coldness and then I was swallowed by a Stygian monster."

An image of a mythical beast; a dragon, or a chimera, popped into her head. "What sort of creature was that?"

"Not a creature. Darkness. All consuming darkness. Not heaven, not hell, just nothing. Nothing, until I was released back into the world. I found myself wandering among the cemetery where we met."

A heaviness blanketed her chest, smothering her heart. Why were all the good ones either taken, or not interested in women; or–

Or dead. Now she could add 'dead' to that list.

"I suppose, since we're being completely honest, that I might as well tell you I've never felt such an attraction to a man like I do to you." She blew a puff of air. "And now I find out that you're a ghost."

He sighed. "Nobody's perfect, I suppose."

"Something must have happened to make you stuck on earth. I mean, it sounds like you were murdered. Did you have any enemies when you were alive?"

His eyes narrowed in thought. "You know, I haven't touched a person since I changed into this form. But I have a feeling that if I were to touch you, you might be able to see what happened behind my back. Would you care to witness it?"

Maisie's breath caught in her throat. "I've never been touched by a spirit. I'd love to try."

Amatus glided across the floor towards her, and she was thankful that the skeletal features did not overlay his face any more; helping to uncover the truth about his death would require a strong suspension of disbelief on her part. Thinking of him as a ghost was too distracting. In her mind, she focused on him being a young attractive man in the prime of his health.

As he touched her, a cool sting transmitted from his hand to her bare shoulder, which was still exposed above her skimpy party dress. There was a warm, almost loving expression in his gaze and the cold tingle melted away from her, surpassed by the strong erotic energy between them. What would it feel like if he were to rip off her dress, and-

Her amorous thoughts also melted as the kitchen around her disappeared. She was standing outside in the open air. The sun hung low between leafless branches and a dusting of snow coated the distant hills, but she recognised the lay of the land; this was her hometown in a distant age, during the Roman occupation in England.

She was standing in the midst of the Roman Forum, if she recalled correctly from her schooldays of studying Classical Civilisation, a decade earlier. Open-air markets sold fruit and vegetables, as well as animal carcasses, hanging in clear view of the browsing public. Her attention was drawn to a rectangular building ahead, where ten elaborate marble archways presented an ornate entrance. Curious, she walked under the intricate archways and entered a circular space with a series of rising benches that formed rings around it. It looked too small to be an ampitheatre; this had to be the Comitium, a public space for important political meetings, or other events. Only for now, the space was occupied in an entirely different manner. Even at first glance, she knew from the scenes of lust and debauchery that a fertility ritual was taking place.

"This is the festival of Lupercalia. We celebrate it on February the fifteenth every year in honour of the fertility god Lupercus." Amatus' disembodied voice spoke at a point in front of her, though he wasn't visible to her at all.

Two naked men stood side by side on a stone platform, their foreheads smeared with the blood of a sacrificed goat. Nearby a priest, wearing a white toga with a red fold layered over his head, butchered the carcass of the goat with a sharp knife. Maisie was repulsed as the priest handed strips of the poor animal's hide to male revellers in the Comitium.

"Those are februa, a gift from Lupercus."

She wrinkled her nose in disgust. The men, clad only in loin coverings, togas slung low around their waists, or completely naked, ran amok in the open space of the Comitium, whipping any women nearby with the thongs made from the unfortunate goat's hide.

"That's barbarous." She felt close to vomiting. "Poor animal. I'm vegetarian, I disagree with killing animals for meat – but this is even worse."

A flood of emotions swamped her. The conflict of wanting to find out the truth of Amatus' death and disgust at the primitive customs, weighed on her mind. Closing her eyes didn't work either, as it was a paranormal vision in her mind as much as a ghostly scene of the past being played out in front of her.

"We didn't have metal contraptions like that one you use to store food. I can see how that would keep your food fresh. Yes, we killed animals for meat. But also as a sacrifice to our gods to protect us, and also to clothe us and keep ourselves warm."

Guilt stung her. It was an ancestral culture, not one that followed her modern expectations. She took a deep breath to reset her mind and kept watching. "Sorry, Amatus. It's not my place to judge."

"Judge if you like." His tone was gentle. "We brought civilisation to this land, and with that, the freedom to judge. Isn't that the nature of a Republic?"

Imagine a philosophy lesson from a person from a culture she considered more barbarous. She grinned. "Yes, you're absolutely right."

With renewed effort, she concentrated on the scene that played before her, studying the faces of the men and women engaging in their Lupercalia celebrations. It was only then that she noticed him; Amatus was one of the men with his toga slung low around his waist. His bare chest was slim and toned through his youth, though not muscled; she surmised that he wasn't a soldier, or common labourer.

Amatus' omniscient presence in front seemed to know her thoughts. "I was a bard in my lifetime, and a very good one too, even if I say so myself. Some of my work verged on the satirical. Not to the extent of Juvenal's work, I should say, but enough to garner a few gasps in the audience from time to time."

Amatus in the past vision chased after a woman with chestnut brown hair. Maisie looked closer at the Roman woman and gasped. She was the spitting image of herself, a doppelganger. He whipped the woman with the febua, causing her to throw out her bare chest and gasp in ecstasy. As Amatus caught up to her, he seized the woman around her waist and spun her around. They embraced in a passionate kiss and his left hand cupped her right breast and fondled it. The voyeur in Maisie tingled to see such an erotic act in public; more so because the woman was her double.

Amidst the revelry, an older man in his fifties or sixties approached behind Amatus and the mystery brunette. He was well-dressed, clad in a toga that had gold piping along the edges. In one swift move, the man raised his right hand and Maisie saw the sacrificial dagger, still covered in blood, that had been used to butcher the goat. The man plunged the dagger in between Amatus' shoulder blades causing him to throw back his head and gasp. The woman screamed and clasped her hands over her mouth as Amatus began to sink to the ground, blood spurting from his mouth. As he sank in a pool of his own blood, his eyes remained wide and glassy, reflecting the sky above.

The older man then seized the young brunette by her wrist and scooped her up into his arms. She beat him with both fists and kicked out with her legs, but he was too strong as he marched out of the Comitium.

"So that is what happened." Amatus' voice was full of bitterness. Moments later, he materialised before her as the scene of ancient life faded. Maisie blinked to reorient herself in her kitchen.

Amatus let go of her shoulder and placed both hands on his head. He spun on the spot for a moment, lost in his thoughts.

An image of the murderer lingered in her mind. "Who was the man?"

"Brutus. He was my neighbour, and a statesman. He had his eyes on Julia, a freed slave, but she resisted his advances," he said, his voice dark. "Lupercalia, you understand, was a festival for men to choose a woman to couple with for the following year. Often the couples would go on to wed."

Maisie thought of the woman, with an uncanny resemblance to herself. "I wonder what happened to Brutus? Did he go to jail for murdering you, or did he go on to marry that woman who was young enough to be his daughter?"

Amatus cast his eyes downward. "Knowing Brutus, he walked free. He was an influential man, with lots of friends in the courts, and enough money to buy his way out of trouble. On the other hand, I was a bard of moderate means."

Maisie tried her best to clear her mind of the ancient crime scene, but couldn't. It was indelibly imprinted, like after watching a movie. "What does this mean for you, though? We know why you're stuck, walking the earth, but I wonder why it's only now that you're able to talk to someone?"

He stroked his chin, his eyes narrowed. "That place where you met me. Those people, the ones wearing yellow hats and strange armour, bright yellow tunics."

She raised her eyebrows. "You mean, the archaeologists? They study the past, you know, digging up old houses and graves and stuff."

A shadow passed over his face. "They dug up my bones. I'm sure of it. I watched them working, but I didn't make the connection, until now."

Her mouth dropped open. "You mean, Mylo died on your grave?"

His grey expression dissipated. "By Jove, that's it! Your dog! Lupercal was watching. He took that as a sacrifice. Dogs and goats are the animals associated with Lupercalia. They were often sacrificed to worship the fertility god."

Maisie recoiled. "You mean my dog had to die in order for you to be seen by someone?"

"Not just anyone. My true love. Did you get a good look at my lover, in my former lifetime, Julia?"

She nodded.

"You and she are one. I'm sure of it. You share the same soul. Two different lifetimes, one soul."

She swallowed a dry lump in her throat. He was talking about reincarnation. Could that really be the explanation; that she was the woman, Julia, in a past lifetime? Such a notion was hard to wrap her head around. At the same time, it made sense. Deep down, in a part of her subconscious mind that had lain dormant for the longest time, she understood.

Amatus' eyes sparkled with an ethereal light. "Don't you see? This is our chance that we didn't have in our lifetime before. Lupercal has seen fit to grant us our affectio maritalis."

Maisie understood. "I have a white dress that would be perfect for the occasion."

"Do you have a red belt? Something that can be tied in a knot of Hercules?"

She nodded with a grin. "Yes, a red silk rope that would work."

"Then, let us not waste any further time. I will ready myself and be back soon."

With that, Amatus disappeared, as if he had been nothing more than a figment of her imagination.

Maisie hurried upstairs and changed into her white dress. It was a simple tunic-style gown that she had worn to a formal dinner a few years back. After watching a tutorial online about how to fasten a knot of Hercules, her fingers were nimble, working the red silk rope. Had she sourced an untapped reserve of ancient knowledge from deep within her mind to be able to fasten one on the first attempt? Maybe. It was an important occasion, after all. Her wedding day.

Crazy. If her self of a few hours previously could have known what awaited in the hours after finishing a date with Keth-Kyle-Kevin, she never would have believed it. Getting married to her long lost love from two thousand years ago on the ancient festival day of Lupercalia, on the fifteenth of February, was in the realms of impossibly mind-blowing stuff. She tossed her head, revelling in the sense of romantic disbelief. Maisie applied red lipstick and drew two dark lines of kohl on her upper eyelids, giving herself a simplistic spartan beauty. She pinned her mop of windswept hair up in a top knot in a way that was hopefully befitting of a soon to be betrothed Roman lady.

As she walked down the stairs, her front door swept open and curling fog spiralled into her hallway. Amatus entered and beside him walked a familiar, small, white miniature schnauzer. The little dog was surrounded by a faint glow and walked with a spring in his step that she hadn't seen for many years.

"Mylo." She marvelled at her pet, then turned to Amatus in amazement. "You brought my dog back to life?"

"Only his spirit. He is my wedding procession. Traditionally, I would have led my family to your house, but he is all I have."

"He's my family, so it counts," she smiled.

"I come here to formally ask you if you will grant me affectio maritalis?" Amatus extended his right hand, palm facing up.

Maisie descended the last step of her staircase and placed her right hand within his palm and he closed his faintly glowing fingers around hers. "I do."

His face stretched into a wide grin. "Then we are wed. We pledge to live with each other for eternity."

Mylo bounded away from Amatus' side and made a circle around the happy couple, wagging his tail. Maisie giggled with delight as she watched her dog enjoying the perks of his youth once more in death. He dashed across to the bundle of white fur that lay in his dog bed and as she watched in wonder, his spirit circled his body three times before settling down in the dog bed. The small dog in the pet bed trembled before getting unsteadily to his feet. Maisie whimpered.

"What – what on earth?"

Mylo was alive.

Maisie turned to Amatus, both hands cupping her nose and mouth.

"He's alive. What did you do?" she gasped.

"It's simple. He sacrificed himself to me, but it wasn't his time. He still has another few years of life left in him. Lupercal gave him his life back because we too gave a sacrifice to him. We gave him the gift of our union," he explained.

"So, then what happens to you?"

"No more wandering the earth, haunting the site of my grave. No more watching people come and go, while I float unnoticed and unheard. You have set me free."

Even as he spoke, he began to glitter and fade, swallowed by the swirling fog.

"Aren't we meant to be together for eternity?" Her voice was small and strained.

"Yes, and I will wait for you in the Elysian Fields until you join me, when it is your time."

His voice grew fainter. "Brutus will never have you again."

Barely an echo. "You are mine."

A mere whisper. "And I am yours."

Gone. Only the wind.

"Wait for me," she shouted out her front door.

She would keep herself for him. No marriage to any Kevin, or Keith, or Kyle, or anyone else. She was already betrothed, affectio maritalis, to her one true love Amatus.

Her special Valentine's Day Valentino.

"Lupercalia blessings, my love," she shouted to the flickering dawn on the horizon. And the dawn whispered back:

I love you my Julia. My Julia.

A gruff voice from next door cut through the air. "Shut up! I'm trying to sleep."

6

Brocken Spectre

Troy dipped his paintbrush in the small jar of water and swirled it around to clean the brush. What a gorgeous morning it was, the natural beauty of dawn enhanced by the mist. The colours were perfect for painting. The hill was partly enveloped by the mist, and with the sun rising behind him, it threw the landscape into an array of colours. The grass appeared a duck-egg blue, while the mist swirled with pink and purple hues.

He squirted a dot of red onto his palette, then mixed it with a splash of white to make pink. Next, he added a smudge of blue to make indigo. He flicked his eyes upwards to the mist, then laid them down again on his palette. The colour mixing looked right for a change. He smiled to himself, then blotted his brush on a tissue to apply just the smallest touch to the board on his easel.

Perfect.

Troy stood up from his folding travel seat to peer down the hill. He needed to get the texture of the grass and shrubbery right, or the landscape scene would look too cartoonish; and he wanted to practise Realism in his composition.

The peak of a faraway hill emerged as the mist parted on either side of it. As the sun rose behind him, a circular rainbow appeared on top of the peak with the shadow of a person in the centre.

This made him gasp. "An angel."

He stooped to grab his camera from his bag, keeping his eye on the shadow within the rainbow, and noticed that the figure stooped as he did. When he stood up, the figure also stood in sync with him. He raised his hand and waved, and the figure waved back.

Troy laughed. "It's me."

It seemed the sun had projected his shadow far across the grassy valley, placing it on top of the neighbouring hill. The phenomenon had lost its magic, but not its charm. He snapped a picture on his camera to refer back to later, then sat back down on his travel chair to add the rainbow and shadow to his painting.

After he had detailed the rings of red, orange, yellow and blue encircling his own shadowy figure, he paused for a sip of water and to search on his phone for such a phenomenon, if his phone signal would allow him.

"Circular rainbow with shadow inside on top of a hill," he said aloud as he typed.

It seemed what he had encountered was called a 'Brocken spectre'. Funny name, considering there was nothing supernatural about such a natural, but rare occurrence.

Troy turned his attention back to the Brocken spectre. The rainbow had diminished a little as the mist began to clear, but he could still see his own shadowy figure in the middle. For fun, he raised his hand and waved at it, enjoying his shadow waving back.

"Ah, funny stuff. Probably the best painting I'll do all year," he mused out loud. Part of the fun of painting alone was that he could talk to himself; it warded off the loneliness. He hummed a tune as he started packing up his paints and brushes, leaving the board and easel until the end.

The wind whispered behind him, stirring the hairs on the back of his neck. A sixth sense made him glance across to the circular rainbow once more.

The Brocken spectre waved at him.

Troy yelped. He watched, transfixed in horror, as the shadowy figure moved within the mist. A person began to emerge, too solid to be a shadow, and definitely not *his* shadow.

He blinked and rubbed his eyes. He wasn't seeing things. In fact, it was quite simple. A hillwalker had probably been walking in the mist and happened to be passing by when the Brocken spectre appeared. Yes, that was it; merely a coincidence.

He shivered as the wind picked up, chilling the nape of his neck and along his back. Too much time painting alone and getting the heebie-jeebics. Bag in one hand, board and folded-down easel in the other, Troy set off along the grassy path towards the carpark.

One last look back wouldn't hurt, just to confirm that a hillwalker had emerged from the mist.

Troy turned back.

The figure walked across the grassy slope, far across the valley, but with a definite stride. He presumed the person to be a man from the height and build; slim, but with broad shoulders, and he had a strange gait, marching in a robotic way, swinging both arms like a badly animated computer graphic. Whoever the person was, was heading in his direction.

Troy sped up and broke into a run, not looking back anymore as he hurried into his car.

***

His Tuesday evening art class after work was busier than usual with new faces. Troy had never seen the community centre so packed. There was an elderly woman who had never been there before, probably taking up a hobby in her retirement, and a young East Asian woman who looked to be a student, maybe studying art. His eyes scanned the other faces and stopped on a man who looked to be in his mid-twenties, his breath catching in his chest.

The man was exceptionally handsome; like a more attractive photo negative version of himself, in a way. Troy had light brown, wavy hair, compared with the man's floppy black hair that fell forward over his forehead, and whereas Troy had pale blue, almost glacial eyes, the man's deep, dark, expressive eyes were soulful beyond his youth. Unlike his own sturdy build, the man had a delicate, fragile frame, like that of a model. As Troy studied him, the man looked up from his board and locked eyes with him. A soft half-smile rose on the man's face.

Heat crept into Troy's face and he looked down at his feet, before regaining his composure, and looking back to the man, who continued to smile at him.

Oh God, what was happening to him? He had never felt an attraction to other men before. Not that he had felt much attraction to anyone, in fact. He'd had one serious relationship once, but had felt relief when Heidi had decided to break things off after three months. Why had he felt relief? He wrinkled his nose at the recollection. Too shallow. She had no appreciation of art, or museums, or literature; or anything of cultural value. Heidi enjoyed shopping and looking good, getting coppery highlights in her dark hair reapplied every six weeks, wearing horrible bright talons on her fingernails, and false eyelashes that looked like hairy caterpillars. Honestly, he had only dated her because she had pursued him, bragging about how he was her 'sensitive dork'. Conversation with her had been limited to Heidi complaining about everyone she knew, or the latest dating show. Dull, boring and vacuous. Even sex with her felt like he had been fucking a mannequin. The final straw had been when she had demanded that he paint her, to which he had been adamant about how he only painted landscapes. Her ego bruised, she had dumped him, and he had shrugged.

But now?

Who was the new man in the class?

Troy stood up, and before his brain could get itself out of sleep-mode, his feet propelled him in a beeline towards the mystery man.

"Hello." Troy loomed over the man. "I'm Troy. You're new here, right?"

The man's gaze rose slowly, his wide, deep-set eyes even more intense up close as they settled on Troy's face. "Yes, this is my first time. My name's Gilbert."

As Gilbert peered up at him, he was struck by the vulnerability of the man. There was a fragility about Gilbert, something Troy sensed, but couldn't pinpoint. He gulped. He had never felt such a desire to paint anyone before as he did when he watched Gilbert sitting in front of him. Everything about him was intriguing; his rough woollen jumper, knitted in alternating light and grey lines, that contrasted harshly against his smooth, pale skin, and those intense eyes that peered out from under a heavy, dark fringe.

He had never felt such desire to kiss him either.

"So, do you like art, then?"

What a *stupid* thing to ask; Troy bit his own lip, trying to quell the burning feeling rising in his cheeks. Gilbert was at an art class; of *course* he liked art.

"I'm not sure. I've never painted before. I thought I would try something different."

Gilbert's response gave him the boost of confidence he needed. "Well, I could give you pointers, if you like. Do you mind if I see what you've done?"

Gilbert turned his board around and Troy recoiled.

Garish black lines depicted the outline of a tragic-looking figure, painted in dark grey with black highlighting, as though the person was in shadow. There was a mop of black hair, and eyes that had been depicted as two black rectangles, made with dashes applied by a wide-bristled brush. The nose was simplistic, looking like an upside-down number seven. A single black arch created a pouting mouth, and two uneven parentheses on either side of the downturned mouth formed frown lines. The shoulders were broad, and wavy horizontal lines on the torso gave the impression that the figure was wearing a stripy jumper. There was no detailing at all on the legs or head, they were simply painted in a uniform dark grey in straight lines with no outline of hips, making Troy think it was supposed to imply a man. Behind the man, a halo of black and grey lines looped like arches that framed him against a single patch of fading light. It looked like something a young child, only learning to paint, would create, except the brush strokes showed a steady, purposeful hand. Gilbert had intended to paint the figure that way. Troy had never seen anything so *ugly*.

"That's – very interesting," he said, emphasising the latter word in a way he hoped showed enthusiasm and not insult.

"Thank you," said Gilbert, his voice neutral.

"You have a talent for painting," Troy went on. Damn his tongue, giving compliments to Gilbert that weren't merited.

"I appreciate that," Gilbert replied, still in a soft tone.

An awkward silence fell between them, though Troy took a moment to appreciate Gilbert's beauty instead of his ugly painting. There was no way he had been painting *himself* in the monotone work, was there? The floppy black hair, and stripy jumper seemed to hint that it was a crude self-portrait. There was no way he could possibly see himself in such a dark, ugly, garish manner, was there?

"Well, I better get back to my own work. It was nice to meet you," Troy finished.

Damn it; there just wasn't any easy way to ask Gilbert out for a drink after class. It would have been too presumptuous. At the same time, he didn't want to miss any opening he had to get to know the new mysterious addition to the art class. Plus, if there was any way he could give him tips about creating less disturbing paintings, then that would be a boon too.

***

It was no use; he simply had no imagination. Troy threw his paintbrush down onto the grass. He was going to have to admit defeat. With a big sigh, he clapped both hands over his face and massaged his cheeks with his fingers, pressing his palms into his chin.

There was no mist over the hills today, and therefore no appearance of the rare Brocken spectre phenomenon that he had seen the previous day. The circular rainbow that he had painted on his board seemed forced – and fake. Even worse, the shadowy figure within it seemed contrived, somehow. How ironic that he was an artist, yet he couldn't paint anything from imagination. He needed to be inspired by a scene in front of him, otherwise his mind was as blank a canvas as the board that awaited his paintbrush.

His mind jumped to the crude black and grey lines that Gilbert had painted on his own board in art class the previous afternoon. It had been Gilbert's first class, and yet he painted with such confidence. It didn't matter that Troy found Gilbert's work *ugly*; the fact was, Gilbert had a distinct *voice*. His work stood out for its ugly, bold craftsmanship. If nothing else, he made a bold artistic statement.

Troy swooped down and snatched up his paintbrush. He squirted a dash of black onto his palette and added a dot of white to mix dark grey. He then enhanced the figure in the centre of the circular rainbow, adding a slim, tall physique and broad shoulders. He slipped the cover off his fine-detail brush and added a touch of black highlighting to the Brocken spectre's face, adding high cheekbones and a chiselled jawline, as well as a shock of black, floppy hair falling forwards over the brow. As with every painting he did, Troy took a moment to look elsewhere and clear his mind of his artistic vision, in order to be an objective judge of its quality. He stood up, stretched, and watched the fast-moving clouds for a few minutes, before returning his gaze to his board.

Ugly.

Troy gagged as he surveyed the black painted image of the Brocken spectre he had created. It was ugly. Worse than ugly; hideous. It was as though Gilbert's hand had possessed his body for a few minutes while he created the ghastly figure. Crude black lines distorted the face and gave it features more like a carved pumpkin for Halloween rather than a face. Clearly Gilbert had been his muse, in the sense that he had been thinking of the attractive mystery man in his art class while he created the figure, but the results had been a disaster.

Unsure of what to do, Troy dipped his paintbrush in water and smudged the bristles across his creation's face. The paint was still wet; it would be easy to erase. He lifted the brush away and looked.

No change.

Strange. Watercolour paint should have been easy to fix before it dried; how uncanny that it was unfixable. He had no choice but to paint the whole of the Brocken spectre's face black and start again later.

***

Working in his garage wasn't ideal, but Troy had no spare room in his house for an art studio. At least it provided a lot of light when the door was raised, and plenty of inspiration from the robins that visited his garden, adding interest to the wintery bushes.

Not that he was interested in painting robins today. After a whole day's break, he felt ready to revisit his latest Brocken spectre painting.

As he slid it out of the bag, Troy recoiled, feeling his lip twitch upwards in disgust. The garish lines still showed, as though he hadn't repainted the whole face.

Maybe going back to the original source would be a better inspiration. He pulled out the original painting he had done, on the day the Brocken spectre had appeared, for comparison's sake.

Was it his imagination, or were there faint black lines on the figure's face? He definitely hadn't painted any at the time. Troy bent low, observing the painting close enough that his nose almost touched the board. Yes. It was undeniable. The Brocken spectre had fine lines, crude black lines, marking out its features.

He set the painting down with a sigh. Apart from the two Brocken spectre works, he hadn't created anything else in the last few days. His next art class was that evening. If he didn't come up with any inspiration for a new nature scene before then, he would see if an idea might pop to mind in his class. Would Gilbert be there? His heart seemed to speed up a beat at the thought of the new, gorgeous classmate.

Troy grabbed the handle of the garage door, ready to shut up his workshop for the day and get ready for work. The weak wintery sun shone through the birch tree in his neighbour's garden opposite. The silhouette of a tall, slender man was briefly outlined by a ray of light, shown between the branches of the tree. He did a double take, studying the tree more closely. Nonsense; there was no such figure, not even a shadow that could be interpreted as a person.

Not enough coffee, perhaps. He scratched his head and slammed the garage door down, a bit harder than intended, then locked it. Getting his mind off the Brocken spectre was the utmost priority, so that a new inspiration could take its place.

***

Traffic really hadn't been bad for rush hour Thursday, and Troy made it to his art class early. The art teacher was still setting up all the boards and palettes for everyone, so he took a moment to look at the paintings from the last group who had taken the classes at the community centre. Maybe a spark of inspiration would come from the scenes they had painted.

Movement from the unlit corridor outside the room caught his eye, and Troy snapped his head to the left to see a shadowy figure striding towards the class. His heart thundered in his ribcage as he noted the broad shoulders and slender physique like the Brocken spectre he had seen two days ago. As the figure drew nearer, and a sliver of light from the classroom began to highlight the person's facial features, Troy saw two black rectangles for eyes, a sharp, L-shaped nose and an upturned crescent mouth. He choked on his own saliva as a wet splutter rattled out of his mouth, and took a step backwards, bumping against the art supply cupboard behind him.

A moment later, the bright light of the classroom vanquished any shadows and he saw Gilbert enter the class. There were no rectangular eyes, only Gilbert's wide set dark and soulful ones. His straight nose didn't look like an upside down seven, and his mouth wasn't set in a frown; he had a naturally downturned mouth that gave him a serious, intelligent disposition that Troy found very appealing. Dare he say, *sexy*.

"Hello Troy," said Gilbert, in his usual soft manner.

Gilbert remembered his name. Troy sniffed to compose himself. "Er, hello Gilbert. I'm glad to see you back at class."

Oh no. Was that too presumptuous? Would Gilbert know he was interested in him? He fought to quell the heat rising in his face.

He was distracted from his neurotic thoughts by other people entering the class and taking up their spots, though noticed that Gilbert's eyes held his gaze for a count of three; the amount of time it took for his mouth to form a lopsided smile, before he turned towards his own place in the class. So *sexy*.

"Okay everyone, I hope to find you all well this evening?" The teacher's voice torpedoed his thoughts, which he was immensely grateful for. He sat at his place and crossed his legs, focusing on the single red rose that the teacher had set beside his board to distract himself.

"Today we're going to learn pointillism. I have given you all roses, since it will be Valentine's Day tomorrow, and you'll see that I have given you all a pack of fine-tipped paint pens to work with for this class. If I could have all your attention on my board, I'll demonstrate what pointillism is," said the teacher.

As everyone's eyes heads turned towards the teacher's board, Troy's focus slid sideways towards Gilbert, who sat by the door. Gilbert's intense dark eyes gazed right towards him, although his face was inclined towards the teacher. As Troy continued to stare at him, Gilbert's head turned to match his gaze and they locked eyes. A slow smile spread over Gilbert's face, close-lipped, but knowing and Troy couldn't help responding, his lips peeling apart into a wide smile.

What was behind that knowing smile? Troy wanted to walk across the room, cup his hands around Gilbert's face, and press his open mouth against his. He wanted to push his tongue into Gilbert's mouth. He wanted to run his hands through his floppy black hair.

"Alright, so as you can see, it's time consuming, but the end result is quite satisfying. You can achieve a surprising amount of detail by varying the spacing of the dots you apply," the teacher said. Troy snapped back to attention and looked at the front. Pointillism? Dots? He looked at the detail in the rose head impression the teacher had dotted on the board and back to his own rose, next to his board. Piece of cake.

Or maybe not. His attempt at pointillism resembled a young child's dot to dot efforts rather than a somewhat skilled art hobbyist. Troy sighed. Wonder how everyone else was getting along with pointillism?

His feet led him without thought. Gilbert looked up as he approached and lifted his pen off his board to let Troy see his work.

Horrible. An abomination. The rose Gilbert had created looked like a grotesque Titan arum plant rather than a rose. He had chosen to depict it entirely in black ink rather than vibrant red and green hues. Troy couldn't help wrinkling his nose, the ghastly picture imprinted on his eyeballs even when he blinked his eyes closed.

"What do you think?" A hopeful look glinted in those wide, dark eyes as Gilbert turned to him.

Troy was rooted to the spot, transfixed by the ugliness of Gilbert's creation. He opened his mouth, shut it, opened it again and his bottom lip quivered in an attempt to filter himself.

"I think it's awful. It has an ugly, gothic quality, like the board itself is actually rotting," he said with a sniff.

Gilbert's face fell, and his hand, still holding the pen, dropped to his side.

A sting of surprise, like a wasp piercing his arm, jolted Troy as Gilbert hung his head. His chest heaved – once, twice – and realised with a stab of guilt that Gilbert was crying.

"Oh shit, mate, I'm so sorry. I didn't mean to be so harsh," Troy offered.

God, he was pathetic. He was such a bastard. He rubbed his face, thinking fast, as more sobs rocked Gilbert's body.

"Um, that was a really shitty thing to say. I'm so sorry. You're just learning, and I had no business saying that." Troy set his hand, tentatively, on Gilbert's shoulder.

Gilbert surprised him again by grabbing his hand and giving a reassuring squeeze. He looked up, his long eyelashes dripping with tears, his eyebrows arched in despair.

"Nobody has ever been so honest with me before. Thank you for speaking the truth," he sobbed.

Troy rubbed his shoulder. "No, it wasn't honesty. It was anger. Your picture made me so angry. I shouldn't have said that. There was no call for it."

"But if you'd said anything else, you would have been lying. Everyone, my whole life, told me lies. You're the first person who hasn't. You're the first person who has respected me."

Troy gulped. What a depressing thought. No wonder Gilbert seemed so fragile and vulnerable – because he was. Had he really been lied to and let down by everyone he knew?

He glanced around at the other students. Everyone was too busy with their own pictures to notice or care about the small scene that he had created by making Gilbert cry. Even the teacher busied about at the front of the class preparing materials for the next class.

"Um, would you like to get out of here? There's a quiet pub near here where we could talk things through? I'd really feel better if I could say sorry properly by buying you a drink."

Gilbert smiled and wiped away his tears with the back of his hand. "That sounds great."

***

Interesting rebranding choice for the pub that had formerly been called *The Goat and Duck*. Under the new management it had been renamed *The Brocken Arms*. Troy smirked to himself as he led Gilbert through the double doors. It seemed an appropriate nod to his recent encounter with the Brocken spectre and his Artist block that had followed, a quiet lull in his painting inspiration that would hopefully prove to be short-lived.

They approached the bar. "What would you like? It's on me," Troy said.

Gilbert sucked air in through both nostrils, his chest expanding, as he perused the drinks behind the bar. "I'll have a Double Ghost IPA."

Intriguing. Gilbert was becoming more appealing by the minute.

"I think I'll try one of those myself." He turned to the barman. "Two Double Ghosts, please."

They took their drinks and walked to a quiet booth. Troy was pleased to see that the new management hadn't renovated the interior; the old-fashioned wooden booths that looked like church pews still remained. Troy slid into the booth first, expecting Gilbert to sit opposite him, but was pleasantly surprised when Gilbert sat next to him, their upper arms touching.

Gilbert took a sip of his drink, his tongue darting out to lick froth off his upper lip. Troy's gaze lingered on Gilbert's mouth while he swallowed a gulp of his own drink.

"Do you know the history behind the name of this IPA? It's named after the ghosts of ships that were lost in Southwold."

Troy laughed. "Perfect for Halloween. We should've got passionfruit liqueur cocktails since it's Valentine's Day tomorrow."

Gilbert chortled. When the laughter between them faded, their eyes locked. Troy felt as though his gaze would never leave Gilbert's flawless face.

"I'm really glad we came here instead of staying in class," Gilbert said.

"Me too. I was going nowhere slowly with that pointillism," Troy added. "In fact, I'm having complete Artist's Block at the moment. I need to find a new inspiration."

Had their faces moved closer together? Gilbert's eyes were mesmerising, his expression hypnotic. Maybe just a notch.

Troy wasn't sure who initiated the kiss; suddenly his lips were locked with Gilbert's. He closed his eyes, delighting in the beeswax taste on Gilbert's lips and the faint smell of mint body wash from his skin. How lucky he was that Gilbert found him attractive too; he wanted to savour every moment, to remember it forever.

They pulled apart a few minutes later, both breathing heavily. Gilbert sipped his drink, but Troy didn't, not wanting anything to wash away the taste of their kiss.

"What do you think would help you get through your Artist's Block?" Gilbert's eyes were innocent and enquiring.

He shrugged. "I seem to only be able to paint things if they're in front of me. I can't seem to be able to paint things from imagination. I like going up to the hills near here and painting the morning landscape, just when the sun is rising. But I saw the most amazing thing recently, and it seems to have killed my artistic sense."

Gilbert tilted his head. "What did you see?"

"It was a shadow inside a circular rainbow. *My* shadow. I looked it up. It's a phenomenon called a Brocken spectre."

"How did that give you Artist's Block?"

Troy looked down at the table, picturing the Brocken spectre. "I don't know exactly. I was able to paint it at the time, but that's the weird thing. Even after I moved, the shadow in the middle remained. I think someone else was inside the circular rainbow, and it wasn't my shadow I painted after all."

Gilbert raised his eyebrows. "Was it something to do with the fact that you painted someone else instead of your own shadow, like you thought, that made you lose your artistic sense?"

What an interesting thought. It hadn't occurred to Troy that maybe that was the case. If the shadow had been his own, he wouldn't have been able to paint it; when he sat down at his easel, he had moved away from the focal point of where the sun hit his back, creating the Brocken spectre through the mist. Logically, that meant, he had painted someone else who had been within the mist, appearing as a shadow.

Had the mystery figure in the mist 'stolen' his artistic skill?

Troy's thoughts dived back to the change in his painting, when he had observed it that morning in his garage. Faint black lines seemed to have manifested on the Brocken spectre's face; lines that he hadn't painted. A chill seized him, like rigor mortis in his shoulders and back. He sat up stiff, staring ahead into space, but thinking of the figure moving in the mist, two days ago, on that sunlit Tuesday morning. The painting had changed to look more like the painting Gilbert had created in art class on Tuesday evening.

His head inched round, slowly, towards Gilbert. Gilbert watched him with a blank expression. Not emotive in any way, just benign.

Troy unclenched his jaw, which suddenly felt so stiff. "I never saw you in art class before. What made you decide to come?"

Gilbert twitched his shoulder upwards in a one-sided shrug. "I'd actually been thinking about becoming an artist's model, you know, for some more cash. But then I decided that I wanted to try and paint instead."

The muscles in Troy's neck and jaw were tight as he talked. "Do you live round here? I've never seen you about before."

Gilbert blinked as he paused in thought. "I guess so. I've lived here and there over the years, but you know the funny thing? I don't actually remember where I live."

What on earth did that mean? As if sensing Troy's apprehension, Gilbert let out a chortle that was tinged with fear, rather than mirth.

"What do you mean? How can you not remember where you live?"

His flawless face contorted as he struggled to recall. "I don't know. I really don't. I came to class on Tuesday because it was important to me, and again today for the same reason. In between, things have been kind of a blur."

That didn't make any sense. Troy shifted in his seat, putting a hand's width gap between them. Gilbert didn't seem to have noticed as he appeared to be concentrating in thought.

"Things can't *just* be a blur, unless you're suffering from amnesia, or are *on* something. But you seem quite lucid to me," Troy conjectured.

Gilbert. Garish lines. Bad art.

"I don't know." Gilbert swept both hands through his hair, pulling it back off his handsome face. "I remember everything clearly about coming to art class and being here with you. But apart from that, it's all just swirling mist."

Garish lines. Gilbert.

"What did you say? The parts you can't remember are like swirling mist?"

"I think so. I mean, it's like in between art class, I'm just walking about lost in swirling mist. I really can't remember."

The effect was immediate. Gilbert's words tore through Troy's brain, ripped down his body and seared into his stomach, making him feel sick. Sick to the core.

"I'm sorry, Gilbert, I'm feeling really ill. I have to go. Please excuse me."

***

An oppressive mist swirled as Gilbert hurried, lost in the marshes. The posey of roses he carried was wilted from his efforts trudging through the brackish water.

Gilbert's black and grey jumper clung to him with sweat. He wiped his damp hair back off his forehead with one sleeve and looked back over his shoulder, his face pale and panicked. Petals dropped from his flowers as he struggled along, his feet making a popping noise with each step in the suction from the mud below the brackish water.

Distracted from constantly looking back, he stumbled and fell forwards, landing in the water with a wet splash. His posey fell beside him, the delicate, red petals coated in dark, brackish mud.

Footsteps behind Gilbert grew louder. A hand emerged from the heavy mist and pushed Gilbert's head down into the murky pool. A strong, stocky man, cast in shadow by the mist, held his head under the water until he stopped struggling and lay, face down, in the black water. As quickly as the pursuer had emerged from the mist, he disappeared; swift and silent.

Troy woke up in a cold sweat. The nightmare had been so vivid, and so real. What if the dream was showing him events that had really happened? Could Gilbert really have been murdered out in the marshes, by a killer hidden in the mist?

He had to know. Like a bomb going off in his mind, Troy's Artist Block had been simultaneously vanquished as his curiosity about Gilbert's situation was piqued. If Gilbert wasn't about to suffer a terrible fate, then he was sure the dream had shown him the truth of an unsolved crime.

Troy got dressed in a rush and hurried out of his house without breakfast or coffee. He tossed his art supplies into the car and phoned his boss to call in sick for the day. Some things were more important than work; like using his newfound psychic ability to help an innocent victim. The details were almost incomprehensible; either Gilbert was a ghost, or about to become one. He was positive that the Brocken spectre he had seen was Gilbert's spirit coming back around the anniversary of his death, or a manifestation of what was yet to come; a foretelling of doom.

As he passed along the High Street, Troy picked up a posey of red roses from the local florist's, then headed to his usual place to paint the landscape. But this time, his inspiration was different.

Instead of setting up his easel on top of the hill, Troy ventured further down-slope into the swirling mists. The turf underfoot began to get softer and spongier, but his need to know the truth steeled his heart. A ray of sunlight through the clouds ahead guided him.

Close to the brackish water, the like of which he had seen in his dream, he set up his board and got his paints ready. Troy held the posey of red roses over the muddy water. It seemed a waste of a beautiful, perfect bunch to coat them black, but they needed to match the authenticity of his dream. As he stooped to dip them into the murky pool, a shiver wracked his body. The posey was almost like a tribute to someone who had died. Was Gilbert dead? But he had seemed so real, so *solid*. They had even kissed.

"Anything I can help you with?"

Troy swore and spun around at the sound of Gilbert's voice close behind.

Gilbert chuckled. "Sorry. Didn't mean to scare you."

Troy brandished the flowers at Gilbert, his heart thumping a mile a minute. He stared at his perfect, flawless features, unable to speak; unable even to think. His mind burst into a flurry of thought after a brief silence, and he babbled, unfiltered.

"You...I saw your death. I saw you die." The roses shook in his trembling hand. "But you're alive. I've touched you. You can't be dead."

He spun on the spot, his mind struggling to comprehend. "It can't be. It couldn't just have been a dream, could it? But it was so real."

"What dream? What did you see?"

His eyes felt like they would bulge out of his head. "Then it must have been a premonition. The dream must have been a foretelling of your murder."

Gilbert's handsome face twisted with confusion. "Murder? What do you mean?"

Troy seized him by the shoulders. "Run, Gilbert, please run. You aren't safe."

"Aren't safe from who?" Gilbert said, one eyebrow raised.

Troy pushed the posey into his hand. "Please. Just do what I say and run. Someone is coming. I'll hold him off."

"Hold who off?" Gilbert's puzzled expression morphed, his eyes narrowing. "What are you up to? Did you bring someone with you?"

Troy shook his head. Desperation welled; why wasn't Gilbert listening to him? "Just go, now, or you'll be sorry."

Any semblance of confusion had now left Gilbert's face as anger replaced suspicion. "Are you threatening me?"

How was he going to get through to Gilbert that he wasn't safe? "Go. Now. Please! Before it's too late."

Gilbert stepped backwards a few paces, his face mournful, the posey of roses clutched against his chest. Troy was frozen by fear at the sudden realisation; this was the exact pose that Gilbert had depicted in his garish, black-lined painting.

It seemed to happen in slow motion, only because of the fear that seemed to suspend time, but Troy watched transfixed as Gilbert turned and began to trudge quickly away from him through the brackish water. Pain stabbed his broken heart as he watched the look of fear, cast over Gilbert's shoulder, towards him.

No, he wanted to say. No, it isn't me you should be afraid of. But the words wouldn't come out of his mouth.

Gilbert broke into a run, swinging the posey in his hand. A trail of petals fell behind him as he ran, drifting onto the surface of the dark water.

How could Gilbert think that *he* was the dangerous man from the premonition? Troy hurried after him. Despite his incredulity, he felt the need to make sure the foretelling of doom didn't happen.

Gilbert, I'll save you, he wanted to say. But huffing along in the marshes and mist, the words wouldn't come out.

One glance back, as though to say: *Stay away from me!*

A chance to seize upon: Gilbert tripped and fell. Down went the posey of roses, now coated black. Splayed on his front, Gilbert was so helpless as he flailed in the muddy water.

Troy caught up to him and reached out. He had to help him.

Why then was no one else there?

He placed his hand on Gilbert's head. It was as though an alien energy possessed him, operating his body remotely. Instead of pulling Gilbert's head up, he smashed it down into the brackish water and held it. Held it steady. Held it longer.

Held it still.

Gilbert lay, splayed in the pool.

As Troy watched, a faint figure, barely discernible from the surrounding mist, rose up from Gilbert's lifeless form. It turned its rectangular eye sockets towards him for the briefest second, the harsh lines of its face carved in disapproval on the spectral face. Holding a posey of ghostly black roses, the sorrowful figure turned and walked uphill towards a distant circular rainbow, projected by the sun onto the crest of a slope, and disappeared within.

Troy turned back to Gilbert's dead body, lying face down in the muddy water. A sudden giddiness enveloped him as his senses returned. An explosive energy surged through him. This was just what he needed. He was an artist. Through his death, Gilbert had unleashed the pent-up creativity that had been inside him, all along.

All he had to do now was to get his board and easel, paints and brushes. The rest was right there in front of him: Gilbert's dead body in a brackish pool, the Brocken spectre up high in bright sunlight and scattered black petals in between.

It would be his best work.

Ever.

7

Inamorata

Jennifer sat cross-legged on the bathroom floor. She lit the aromatherapy candle and set it down, then held the small, black mirror up to eye level. A deep breath helped to clear her head and calm her nerves. Why did this feel like a last resort?

No room for doubts; this had to work.

If you want to see your future husband, you must buy an Obsidian Mirror. Light a candle below it, at the stroke of midnight on Valentine's Day, look into the mirror and you will see his face behind your shoulder. Psychic Meg, the Guru of Eros' words floated back to her, clear as the day she had given Jennifer the advice, at the Christmas Fayre. The technique was called scrying. With her thirtieth birthday coming up in March, the tiny voice at the back of her mind was starting to grow louder in her ear. *You're nearly thirty – find a husband. If you want a baby, you'll need to do it before you're thirty-five.*

Of course, all of that was bullshit; her logical mind had assuaged her fears by doing the research. The whole 'thirty-five-means-you're-a-geriatric-mum' thing was based on one single survey carried out on two hundred French peasant women in the 1800s. How did a survey done on Victorian peasants have any relevance to the fertility of twenty-first century women? It didn't. But the desperation stuck. Her brain chose to ignore her logical mind in favour of irrational fears: find a husband and get knocked up as soon as possible.

Jennifer stared in the mirror. In the dim candlelight, all she could see were her own eyebags and the pores on her nose. Not very flattering light. At this rate, even if her future husband showed up in the mirror, she would frighten him away with her makeup-less face.

She snorted with laughter and nearly blew out the candle. If anyone saw her, they'd think she was mad. Mad and desperate. Her grin faded. It was actually a rather sad and pathetic thing to do.

Was the mirror even working? She had bought it online. What if it wasn't obsidian? What if she had been ripped off? Would it work if it wasn't the real deal?

No time for doubts. Jennifer leaned closer and stared harder into the small, black mirror.

The wispy smoke from the candle rose upwards, wavering towards the ceiling. In the thick, cinnamon scented smoke, the outline of a round face began to form close behind her left shoulder. Two distinctive, heavy-lidded eyes peered at her, and she saw the faint impression of facial hair: a neatly trimmed moustache and short beard. The man had light curly hair.

Jennifer gasped and spun around. Nobody was behind her.

It had worked.

Had it? Or had it been a trick of the light; all smoke and mirrors, so to speak.

She closed her eyes, holding onto the impression of the man, and a warm, erotic feeling began to overcome her. Focusing on the sensation, Jennifer blew out the candle and walked through to her bedroom; hopefully the mysterious man would visit her dreams.

**

Jennifer jogged along the muddy path, holding onto Cleo's leash in her right hand, while wiping sweat off her brow with her left forearm. Valentine's Day morning was cold and crisp, and she relished having the park to herself, as there were only a few early commuters to contend with.

Her red setter led the way, pulling ahead. As Jennifer struggled in the mud, her trainers squelching, she felt her feet slip out from beneath her. She fell forward, letting go of Cleo's leash, and landed on her hands and knees in the muck.

"Oh, yuck. Great." Jennifer struggled to get up in the slick mud. "Good one, Cleo, thanks for that."

Cleo wagged her tail, her tongue hanging out, with not even an ounce of remorse on her face.

"Can I give you a hand?"

She turned to see a striking man behind her. He wasn't especially tall; maybe only five foot seven or eight, but he had green heavy-lidded eyes and light blonde curly hair. If it wasn't for his neatly trimmed beard and moustache, she would have thought he resembled a grown-up cherub.

Jennifer let the man guide her to her feet, one hand on her arm and the other behind her back.

"Thank you, I appreciate that. My dog thought she was being very clever dragging me down in the mud."

Up close his eyes had tiny flecks of brown threaded through them. For a moment, Jennifer found herself lost in his gaze, then composed herself and turned to look for Cleo. Thankfully the silly dog had got her leash tangled in a bramble. The man fetched Cleo's leash and handed it to her.

"You take care now. Don't let her take you off the beaten path," he joked.

As he grinned at her, Jennifer felt exposed. Something about his pale appearance, and those distinctive eyes, gave her the impression that he could see through her, right into her soul. The man didn't look anywhere other than into her eyes, but she felt naked before his gaze regardless. Finding his gaze almost painful, like looking into the sun for too long, Jennifer let her focus drift downwards to an amulet on a golden chain around his neck. It appeared to be an inverted heart-shape with an infinity symbol threaded horizontally through the middle.

"Interesting necklace." She pointed at the amulet.

He became misty-eyed as he touched it briefly with his fingertips. "I'm a hopeless romantic. This proves it."

With that, he turned and jogged away. Jennifer watched him until he disappeared around the bend in the path, hidden by bushes. The air felt charged. Why did he make such a strong impression on her? She hadn't found him attractive in particular; he was average looking, and definitely not her type, but he was *striking*. His features were memorable. What was it about him that made an impression?

The Obsidian Mirror.

The smoky impression of a man behind her left shoulder. The man's features matched the image she had seen in the mirror while scrying. Could that blonde, blue-eyed stranger really be someone she might end up marrying?

Jennifer shuddered as a chill breezed past her. Standing around in the February air was making her cold. She held tight to Cleo's leash and continued jogging on her way.

***

"Mum, I'm serious. I really think Psychic Meg was onto something. I'm telling you, the man looked exactly like the smoky impression I saw in the Obsidian Mirror."

Jennifer's mum, Michaela, tossed her head. "Oh Jenny, love. You're too impressionable. Psychics are fraudsters. She was only telling you what you wanted to hear."

"But he wasn't even my *type*. If I was trying to conjure up my type, I would've pictured a tall dark and handsome man, maybe wearing glasses."

Michaela blinked at her, her sceptical expression melding into one that was starting to look convinced. "Well, supposing fate did intervene and you met him because of that scrying you did in the mirror – magic – whatever it was. You didn't even exchange phone numbers. How are you ever going to see him again?"

Her mum had a point. Jennifer stroked her chin. "If it's meant to be, then he'll show up again, I imagine."

As if on cue, Jennifer's eyes drifted away from her mum to movement at the entrance of the cocktail bar. The blonde-haired man she had met while jogging walked in and stood for a moment scanning the room.

Jennifer tapped her mum and pointed. "There he is, told you. Still don't believe me? Fate thinks otherwise."

Michaela swivelled around, but the blonde man had disappeared into the throng. "Where? Honestly love, you have such an overactive imagination."

Gah, her mum could be infuriating sometimes.

"I don't need you to believe me." Jennifer necked the rest of her Sex on the Beach in one go. "The mirror showed me the face of my future husband, and it was the very same man who showed up when I was jogging earlier, and now again in this bar. So, what am I doing spending Valentine's Day drinking cocktails with my mum."

She slipped off her bar stool, adjusted her short red dress and wandered in the direction the man had gone. Tottering on her extra high-heeled stilettos, she weaved through the crowd, surveying all the faces along the way. One blonde-haired man caught her eye but he wasn't blonde enough, not curly enough. The more she looked among the faces of the other men in the bar, the more attractive her mystery man seemed to become in comparison. It was as though not finding him among the revellers made him more and more of a forbidden fruit.

Inamorata.

The word reached her ear as a mere whisper on the wind. Jennifer turned. Nobody was close enough to her to have spoken the word to her, and that was besides the fact that they were all caught up in their own conversations.

My inamorata.

She was certain that time; the words had been spoken to her. It was as though the speaker was directing them telepathically into her mind.

Jennifer pushed her way through the entire length of the cocktail bar, then checked the area out the back leading to the toilets, waiting a few moments for anyone coming out of the Men's room. He wasn't there. She was sure her mystery man had evaded her, somehow.

This was frustrating. She hadn't wanted him, hadn't found him to have any kind of sex appeal. But now his mystery created its own kind of animal magnetism. She needed him. Wanted him. Had to find him and get to know him. Had to make him hers.

***

The shopping arcade was full of dangling hearts and twinkling pink lights and the romantic décor kept Jennifer focused on her need to find out more about the mystery blonde man. She wandered through the mall, noting the shop fronts. Psychic Meg the Guru of Eros had rented a pop-up stall in one of the vacant shops, if her online search was anything to go by.

It didn't take long to find it. A neon red sign with an inverted pink heart holding an infinity symbol within led her to Psychic Meg's shop. Inside, the walls were draped with plush red fabric, and red velvet chairs, along with antique coffee tables offered a small waiting area where a sign indicated to scan a QR code and book a slot for a love reading.

Jennifer sat on one of the velvet chairs, feeling a puff of air expelled from the cushion. She booked her slot while she waited, listening to the rumble of voices from within the wooden cabin in the corner, where Psychic Meg held her readings. At Christmas, the shopping mall had used the space as Santa's Grotto, but now, Psychic Meg had left the bare wooden façade, simply hanging a large glittery heart over the door.

A few moments later, a young man left the cabin, casting a bashful sideways glance at Jennifer as he passed. A young male attendant beckoned her into the cabin with a smile.

"Can I get you a tea or a coffee?" he asked.

"Tea with milk and one sugar would be lovely, thanks," she said, tucking her hair behind her ear.

He left through an internal door to one side; Jennifer caught a glimpse of a tea room behind the cabin.

"Hello," said psychic, her long silver hair shining in the cabin light. "You are a familiar face, are you not? I believe I have seen you for a session before?"

Jennifer sat in a red velvet chair facing Psychic Meg. "Yes, I came to see you at your stall in the Christmas Fayre."

Psychic Meg smiled, crinkling her eyes. "What can I do for you today, then?"

"When I saw you, I asked for advice about how to meet my future husband. I followed your advice and bought a scrying mirror, then at the stroke of midnight, I looked in it by candlelight."

Psychic Meg's eyes narrowed with curiosity. "And what you saw was to your satisfaction?"

Jennifer nodded. "I saw the outline of a man in the smoke. Then when I was jogging yesterday, on Valentine's Day morning, I met him."

The Guru of Eros sat back with a satisfied smile, clasping her hands together and placing them on her coffee table. The attendant returned with tea for them both, then left without a word.

"I saw him again last night while I was out at a cocktail bar with my mum, but I lost him in the crowd." Jennifer was embarrassed; it sounded so pathetic when she said it out loud that she had spent Valentine's Day with her single parent mum, and was single and sad herself.

"It seems my advice has been working for you quicker than expected. The results very much depend on the individual. The more desire you have in your heart, the better the chance of results. I can see that this is an important issue for you?" Psychic Meg sat forward, her silvery hair tumbling over her shoulders.

She might as well come clean. "Yes. I'll be thirty next month. I want to meet a man and get pregnant, hopefully within this year."

Psychic Meg poured tea for them both and sipped her own. "You have a strong heart's desire. It burns with pure love. Are you happy with this man, who has come into your life?"

Jennifer hesitated, then pushed the image of a tall, dark and handsome spectacle-wearer out of her head, replacing it with the small, curly blonde man, with his with his heavy-lidded green eyes, beard and moustache. "Yes, I think so."

"Then he shall come back into your life today. So long as your heart is an open door, new love will come and fill it. What will you be doing later today?" The

Guru of Eros ran her finger along the table in a heart shape, drawing an infinity symbol in the middle.

Jennifer pressed her lips together. "Nothing exciting. I have to pick up something for dinner."

Psychic Meg stopped her finger in the middle of the infinity symbol and held it there as she spoke. "Expect to see him there, when you are shopping. If you tell him your intentions, whatever they may be, then you will have success."

What did she mean by 'intentions'? To get married and get knocked up as soon as possible? Such a thing might make a man run a mile away. Jennifer gulped her tea, burning her throat. When Psychic Meg talked of intentions, she must have meant getting the man's number, or asking him on a date.

As she drained her teacup, Jennifer felt dregs in her mouth and pushed them out with her tongue, swilling them to the bottom of the cup with the last drop of tea. She set the teacup down and stared at it in amazement. The tealeaves had formed a dotted heart.

"The universe has delivered an answer to you. The omens are in your favour."

***

How right Psychic Meg had been. If Jennifer had tried to sum it up for anyone, if would have sounded cray-cray. Like, insanely impossible, nah-uh, not believable, this-kind-of-meet-cute-only-happens-in-movies   sort of way.

But it had happened to her.

She had been in the supermarket getting dinner as planned, and aware of Psychic Meg's prophecy only at the back of her mind. She had been holding a punnet of strawberries, and while inspecting one that resembled a large, inverted heart, he had sidled up.

Martin. His name was Martin.

They had laughed about him rescuing her from the muddy jogging mishap and laughed also about the missed opportunity in the cocktail bar.

He had quipped about them repeatedly bumping into each other as a strange coincidence and she had joked about fate.

Dinner had ended up for two, with a spontaneous quickie afterwards on the sofa. After dessert, a marathon sex session had followed. If he hadn't been her type before, he certainly was now.

Jennifer propped herself up on one elbow and looked down at Martin, lying asleep in the bed next to her, and thinking of how erotic the whole evening had been. The duvet was pulled up to his bellybutton, and his bare chest rose and fell in a gentle rhythm as he slept. She glanced at the inverted golden heart, with its infinity symbol, resting on his collar bone as the chain lay loose around his neck. Martin must really believe in true love and destiny like she did. She grinned; she had found another hopeless romantic like herself.

Hopeful. Not a hopeless romantic; hopeful.

She lifted the golden heart to get a closer look.

Was there a faint engraving along the double loops of the infinity symbol? It was hard to read upside down, even when she craned her head.

Martin was in a deep sleep; she was sure it wouldn't wake him if she removed the necklace to look at it more closely. Her deft fingers worked to slide the golden chain around so that she could reach its clasp and unfasten it.

She slipped the amulet off him and inspected it a hand's width away from her nose.

May this soul find its twin and bind them from within.

Hmm. It was a simple message. She had been expecting something much more romantic, like, *I love you to infinity*, or a similar such phrase, given the infinity loop within the heart.

Martin groaned in his sleep and his eyes flickered open, drawing Jennifer's attention. His eyes opened wide as they rested on the chain in her hand.

"What are you doing? Don't take that off!"

Martin snatched the chain. Was it her imagination, or did his hand seem especially pale and ashen as it grabbed the amulet from her hand? Not only pale and ashen, but translucent. She blinked, trying to comprehend the fact that she had seen the golden heart and infinity loop through his balled fist.

He hurriedly fastened the chain back around his neck. Far from being pale, Martin was a flurry of colour; red and flushed from his excitement.

"I'm sorry," she gasped. "I didn't mean any harm. I just wanted to look at it more closely."

His chest heaved as he breathed like he had been running. "I can't lose that. It's worth more than my life."

She rested her eyes on the amulet, then dropped her gaze to the bedsheets. It was horrible to see him panicked. "I wasn't trying to steal it. I'm really sorry, I should have asked."

His breathing steadied, and his flushed face returned to normal. "It's okay. I didn't think you were trying to steal it, and I didn't mean to scare you."

Jennifer gulped, trying to gather her whirlwind of thoughts. "It's my fault. I think I must be still half asleep. I could've sworn your hand was see-through just now when you grabbed the necklace."

Martin's face was solemn as he listened to her. "I guess it's time to come clean with you. I'm not what I seem."

She stared at him. "What are you talking about?"

"It's easier if I show you." He unfastened the golden amulet and held the chain in one hand. The effect was immediate; Jennifer could see through him.

"What is this? Is this some kind of trick?" She climbed out of the bed and took a few steps towards the door.

A sadness swept over him as he shook his head. "It's no trick. The amulet contains some of Psychic Meg's life energy. She shared it with me to fulfil my wish, on my one year anniversary."

"Anniversary? What are you talking about?" Jennifer took another inch towards the door.

"I went to see her last year, just before Valentine's Day. I'd come out of a messy divorce, and wanted to know what the future held for me, in terms of finding a new love. She told me my soul mate was nearby and would come to me soon. She told me we had spent many past lifetimes together, and it was only a matter of time before we met again, in this lifetime."

Jennifer found herself unable to speak, her mouth tethered shut by his words.

"But on the way home from my session with her, my car veered off the road in the rain and hit a tree."

Her voice was unleashed in a torrent of emotions. "Are you saying you're a ghost? But that's ridiculous."

"I don't know what you mean exactly by ghost. If you mean spirit form, then yes, I'm a spirit. Psychic

Meg is as good as her word. She matches up everyone who comes to her for help."

Jennifer inched further away, now standing in the doorway. "I don't understand at all. Is this some kind of scam? Are you up to something with Psychic Meg, a trick to dupe innocent people out of their money? What's in it for you?"

"No trick, only love." He held both hands up, in a pleading gesture, the amulet still dangling from one hand. "Please, Jennifer. Don't you see? You're my one true love that she was talking about. You're my soul mate who has been with me through many past lifetimes."

"Then why are you telling me you're dead?" she cried, her voice wavering.

"I'm not. I never said I was dead. You didn't let me finish. When I had the car accident, my body went into a coma. I'm in the hospital, like a vegetable. But my spirit was set free. I went back to the Guru of Eros for her help, and she lent me her life energy to get my message to you."

***

Valentine's Day had arrived. Should they go out for dinner? No. It wouldn't be much fun having to sip non-alcoholic cocktails anyway, while everyone around her was getting hammered. Jennifer placed a hand on her stomach. The baby was due any day.

Martin walked into the living room at that moment carrying pizza baguettes with a big grin on his face. There was no amulet hanging around his neck; it was framed on the wall above the fireplace instead. He didn't need the life force anymore; he had his own.

After his revelation to her the previous year, his comatose body had opened its eyes the moment he had finished talking. Soul and flesh had reconnected. After a few months of physiotherapy – and Jennifer by his side – he had made a full recovery.

True love had brought him back to the land of the living.

Jennifer beamed. "You read my mind. I was thinking of having a romantic night in, rather than going out. I'm the size of an elephant anyway, I don't have any glamorous maternity clothes that would be suitable for dinner. Besides, Cleo needs to be part of our celebration – after all, she helped to bring us together."

Martin grinned at the red setter, snug beside Jennifer on the sofa. "Spending so much time in the land of spirit has made me shun people, I suppose. They have too much energy. It can get overwhelming," he said.

"I still don't get it. I still don't understand how we were able to have sex when you were in spirit form." Jennifer scratched her head.

"It's simple. Everything in existence is made from a spiritual substance called Akasha. Imagine all the molecules that make up a person. The more concentrated they are, the more solid a person is – the physical self – in other words the human body. Our spirits have less molecules and are kind of like gas. When Psychic Meg lent me some of her energy, she was lending me some of her Akashic life force. Just for a short time only, of course. Too long, and it would've killed her."

Jennifer was silent, thinking. "I wasn't having sex with Psychic Meg's soul, was I? That's creepy."

Martin laughed, throwing his head back. "No honey, don't worry about that. She just lent me some of her Akashic compounds, for a short time. Enough to concentrate my form – and get the deed done."

"I think I finally understand." She let out a long, satisfied sigh. "Well then, what did you have in mind for our first – and last – Valentine's Day as a trio, before three – you, Cleo and I – become four?"

He kissed her stomach, then leaned in and gave her a more passionate one on the lips. "I have the perfect movie in mind for our babymoon."

"Oh?" she teased. "What's that?"

"Ghost," he laughed.

She laughed too and cuddled into his chest, feeling his warm, solid – and very much alive – body.

8

Love you to Death

Had they made the right decision to move into the cottage?

Christine was having second thoughts. It had seemed quaint when the estate agent had showed them around; the fact that it looked like a living museum with its original, nineteenth century stonework and even a thatched roof, had appealed. But now, doubts were creeping in. There was a sadness in the air that made her uneasy. She wrapped her arms around her middle and cradled herself.

"Mummy, is there electricity in this place?"

She looked at her daughter, Joely, her head cocked to one side.

"Yeah, it just looks old, but it has all mod cons – or so the estate agent said," she sighed.

As if to prove a point, Christine switched on the lights. The sadness vanished immediately. Maybe it had been her imagination; all the place needed was some light.

"I'm going out back with dad and Emmet," Joely said, her blonde hair streaming behind her as she ran through the kitchen.

"Okay sweetie," Christine said, half distracted as she pulled open and admired the spacious cupboards in turn.

Alone, she sauntered through the cottage. It was larger than it seemed from outside, as large as the first studio flat she had shared with her husband, Noah, before marriage and kids had come along. The ceilings were a bit low, common in Victorian cottages, but they wouldn't be a bother for them. Noah was five foot ten and she was five foot seven, so thankfully there would be no concussions to welcome them to their new home.

"Hey honey, you should see the back garden." Noah swooped his arms around Christine's waist, bear-hugging her from behind. "Remember the old oak tree beside the apple tree that we saw on the viewing? There's a tyre swing attached. The landlord must have done it knowing we have kids. Isn't that nice? Plus, can you believe there's a scarecrow?"

"A scarecrow?" She peered out the kitchen window, but the dining room extension blocked the view. "There wasn't any when we viewed it. Do you think the landlord put it there to stop the birds eating the apples?"

Christine let her husband lead her into the garden, hand in hand. She was relieved to see that the scarecrow Noah had referred to meant only a wooden post with a branch tied horizontally to make a cross. The cross was dressed in a khaki grey army-surplus style jacket and a black beanie hat had been placed on top of the post as a head.

"I wouldn't say this is so much a scarecrow as a coat stand. Looks like someone left their coat and hat probably after a heavy night out on the lash," she laughed.

She looked closer at the scarecrow. On top of the jacket, a gold chain had been placed with small golden charm dangling from it. At first she thought it was a symbol of an amphora, but on closer inspection she recognised a female symbol of a woman with her arms held above her head, the hands joined to form a circle. A spiral represented her groin in the middle of her vase-shaped body. Christine couldn't say why, but an involuntary shiver seized her body. "Ooh, I don't like the look of that."

Noah shook his head. "Probably belonged to some drunk teenager having a laugh. Far as I know, nobody was renting this cottage for a while before us."

"Can you get rid of it?" She shivered. "I don't even want to touch it."

"What, the necklace, or the whole thing?"

"The whole thing. Whoever put it up did so in bad taste, if you ask me."

Emmet rushed over and grabbed the hem of the scarecrow's coat, swinging around it. "Don't get rid of it, I like it."

Joely joined him, dancing around it. "Yeah, I like it too. Can we keep it? It's kind of Halloweeny."

Christine looked to Noah for his opinion. Noah shrugged his shoulders. "I have no opinion, honestly. But I guess if the kids think it's cool, why not?"

Three against one. Christine turned, with another shudder, and walked back into the cottage.

***

Christine set her tea mug in the sink. The back garden was south-facing, and the butter-yellow sunset mellowed her reservations about the cottage. The sad, charged energy had returned in the hallway, despite Joely and Emmet chasing each other around the place in high spirits, so the natural lighting helped to bring some cheer.

A shadow flashed across the sunset, casting darkness over her for a split second. Had a cloud passed in front of the sun? Maybe an airplane? She looked up from the dishes and saw a dark-haired man wearing a dark grey, army-surplus style jacket and black jeans cross the garden and disappear behind the dining room extension. He was tall and slim, and from the style of his clothing, seemed to be young.

Alarm bells sounded as unease tingled along her back and prickled the hairs on her neck. Instinct told her this wasn't a neighbour, or even an intruder.

"Noah? Can you come here a minute?"

The sound of her husband's feet thudding along the wooden floorboards of the hallway alerted her.

"What is it, hun?"

"There was a young man in the back garden."

His forehead creased. "Really? Hmph. A neighbour, maybe?"

Christine couldn't say how she was so certain, but she shook her head. "I don't think so."

"What did he look like?"

"Well, I only saw the back of him, but he was wearing a grey jacket and black jeans."

Noah twisted the handle of the back door, ready to step outside, but Christine grabbed his arm. "Something is off about the man," she said.

A smirk creased the corners of his mouth. "I'll send him on his way, don't worry. If you're thinking he's drunk, I'll be careful."

She tried to swallow her fear as she watched her husband stride across the back garden in the direction the man had taken. Curious, she slipped into the adjacent dining room and walked to the sliding doors at the end, which gave a full view of the garden. No sign of the man, anywhere. Noah confirmed the lack of an intruder with a shake of his head.

Christine unlocked the sliding doors from the inside and let him back in. "That's weird. Where could he have gone? It's not like there's a back gate."

A voice popped into her head. *He vanished into thin air.*

"Must have legged it over the fence. Probably got lost heading home from the pub," Noah guffawed.

A flurry of feet announced Emmet and Joely and a moment later, the two children appeared in the doorway. "Mum, I'm hungry," Joely whined.

"Dad's got the fish and chips in the oven," Christine answered, still turned towards the garden.

He disappeared. He was a ghost.

"Speaking of which, should be ready now." He kissed Christine on her forehead as he passed her. "Thanks for the reminder before they got burned to a crisp."

The sound of wooden chairs scraping on the wooden floor behind her signalled Joely and Emmet sitting down to wait for their dinner. Christine folded her arms across her chest as she surveyed the garden. The leaves on the apple tree rustled in a gentle evening breeze and the lawn was dappled with golden sunset. She felt the cool air from the garden massage her face through the sliding doors that Noah had left open. It must have been a strong breeze, for the swing on the oak tree began to move. It swung forward, at first just by a finger's length and back into position, before beginning to move at a steadier pace, like a pendulum. Back and forth, by about an arm's length, as though an unseen hand pushed it. Christine shivered before she snatched the door shut and clicked the lock.

"Let's have a TV dinner, kids." She gestured for Joely and Emmet to get up. "We'll save the dining room for Sunday dinner."

She cast a backward glance at the swing as she followed the children towards the living room. Was it her imagination, or did she see the shadow of a dark-haired man riding back and forth on it? Christine blinked and looked again. Just twilight beckoning, and throwing shadows across the lawn. Nothing more. She couldn't let her overactive imagination give her the willies.

Noah brought the fish and chips out on trays and they all tucked into their dinner, with the kids on the floor and Christine with her husband on the sofa.

"Mum, can we decorate the scarecrow with a hockey mask?" Emmet turned to peer up at her.

Christine frowned at her son. "That came out of the blue. Why do you want to do that?"

"Cause tomorrow is Friday the thirteenth," Emmet continued.

"Yeah, mum, we could call the scarecrow, Jason," Joely piped in.

Christine shivered. "You two are so creepy. I can't believe Uncle Ned let you watch that sort of thing when you stayed over at his house last Halloween. I'd prefer to think of Valentine's Day on Saturday rather than Friday the thirteenth."

"Oh – please," Joely whined.

Noah chortled. "We could have a horror-themed Valentine's Day to suit everyone."

"Don't you dare," she joked, jabbing her husband in the arm.

Her laughter faded as a breeze behind her made Christine whip around. She could have sworn she saw a pale figure from the corner of her eye. It was small in stature, with blonde hair and wearing light-coloured clothing as it passed along the hallway towards the dining room.

"What's up, hun?" said Noah.

"Nothing. But can we stop with all the horror talk? I swear I'm starting to see things."

"Like the man in the grey jacket you saw in the garden? Who was he?" Emmet looked at her like butter wouldn't melt.

"You don't miss a trick, seriously," she laughed. As Christine turned back to her dinner, she did so with her head inclined a little, just enough to see the open doorway from the corner of her eye. Just in case.

***

"I'm meant to be asleep. I really shouldn't be talking to you."

Normally, Christine would have respected Emmet's privacy by knocking; after all, he was growing up too fast at twelve. But her spider senses were tingling. There was a serious, almost urgent tone to his words. She turned the handle, opened the door and flicked the light on. Emmet was looking out of his open bedroom window. When the light switched on, he turned with a gasp.

"Mum, you scared the shit out of me!"

"Language, Emmet. Who were you talking to?"

"A friend."

She walked over to the window, but as she approached, within peering distance of the back garden, Emmet clicked the window shut.

Christine noticed he didn't have his mobile in his hand; he hadn't been chatting with one of his school friends. His phone lay on his bedside table.

"It's after midnight. What friend were you talking to at this hour?" She folded her arms across her chest and peered into the garden. Under the moonlit glow, she could see that it was empty.

Emmet shrugged. "He said his name is Ryan."

"Oh?" Christine rubbed her arms. "You don't have any friends called Ryan. Is he new?"

Emmet stared at her with wide, innocent eyes. "Yeah, he's from here, not one of my old friends."

"And what's Ryan doing out at this late hour?" she went on.

He sniffed and rubbed his nose. "He's older than me. He's allowed out late."

Some of Emmet's friends from his Karate club were older than him, so having teenage friends wasn't worrisome to Christine; but none of them stayed out past midnight.

"How did you meet Ryan? We only just moved in yesterday." She tried to keep her tone light, so that Emmet wouldn't close off from her. It wouldn't be good if she revealed her reservations at a potential bad influence in her son's life, so soon in a new area.

"I only just met him. I heard the swing creaking – it woke me up. And there he was."

Her shoulders tensed. "What does he look like, this Ryan?"

Emmet blinked and rubbed his sleepy eyes. "Um, well he's tall. Nearly dad's height. Like five eight or five nine-ish. He's got black hair and he was wearing a dark greyish jacket."

Christine felt her bones freeze. The man in the garden earlier. She had to hide her fear from Emmet so she could get more information. "What did Ryan say to you?"

"He asked me if we were the new family in this cottage and I told him we'd just moved in yesterday. He wanted to know who we were, so I said there's you and dad, me and Joely."

Alarm bells rang in Christine's head. "Why did he want to know who we are?"

"I suppose it's cause he said he used to live here with his mum and dad, but then they moved away," he clarified.

Emmet. Sweet Emmet. Her innocent, naïve son. How could she tell him that he shouldn't have talked to the man, shouldn't have told him so much personal information about their family. She didn't want to frighten him.

She swallowed to wet her throat. "Did Ryan say anything else about himself?"

"Just that he's nineteen and he goes to the community college."

"Nineteen is a bit old to be friends with a twelve year old, honey." Christine smoothed his hair.

Emmet brushed her off with his hand. "Freddy is sixteen and you don't have a problem with him being my friend."

"That's different. Freddy is a karate club friend and your dad and I have met his parents. Ryan is a man, Emmet. I don't like you being friends with a strange nineteen-year-old who comes into our garden at half-twelve at night."

There was a sudden fire in his eyes. "He didn't do any harm, mum. We were just talking. Besides, I told him we shouldn't be talking, and I doubt I'll see him again."

"I wouldn't be so sure. New friends have a way of coming back, especially if he has a connection to this cottage because he used to live here," she said.

Hopefully he didn't die here. Christine forced the intrusive thought away, before it slipped out of her mouth and then neither of them would get back to sleep.

***

Considering the previous day's events, Christine slept well. She woke to find the bed empty, and indeed the whole cottage empty too. Must have meant that Noah had taken the kids out for a walk around the area, or even down to the beach to explore.

Maybe she was coming down with something? It wasn't like her to sleep-in; normally she was up at the crack of dawn and bustling about. She appreciated that they'd been quiet, letting her rest.

A creak on the hallway floorboards roused her from bed; she sat bolt upright and swung her legs over the side, springing to her feet. Any sleepiness left her system in a flood of adrenaline.

"Noah? Is that you? Emmet? Joely? Are you back?"

She swung the bedroom door open and peered into the hallway.

Why did the pools of shadows in the hallway seem so sinister? She could almost see shapes among them; hunched figures, like blackened souls that had given up on their lives, that had succumbed to torture and death.

Where did such a creepy thought spring from? Christine shuddered and switched on the light, chasing any shadows away. She might have imagined dark shapes in the hallway, but she hadn't imagined the creak of floorboards. It hadn't been the old cottage 'settling' either; it had been the unmistakable sound of footsteps on bare floorboards.

The front door rapping nearly made her jump out of her skin. She hurried along the hallway and saw a small, blonde-haired someone standing behind the opaque glass. The sight of the person made her pause in her steps, recalling the flash of blonde-hair and pale, beige clothing that had appeared in the hallway when they had all been eating fish and chips the previous night.

No, there was no way the blonde-haired person was a ghost. She needed to do something to stop such strange thoughts of *ghosts* and *horror* and creepy things in their new cottage. Housewarming blues, that was all. With a renewed spring in her step, Christine answered the door.

"Hello," said the woman, her piercing green eyes remaining wide, even as her grin stretched. She held a homemade pie with a pastry apple leaf decoration in her hands.

"Erm, hi. Can I help you?"

The woman paused, smiling, for a second before answering. "I'm Freya. You must be my new neighbour."

"Oh." She studied the small, smiling woman. With her pretty heart-shaped face, wide green eyes and smattering of freckles over her nose, ordinarily Freya should have seemed friendly. Yet, there was something *off* about her. Christine wanted to pinpoint what it was about the woman that made her feel uncomfortable, but couldn't say what. Freya was diminutive. Her blonde shoulder-length hair was unobtrusive. Her beige floral print dress was benign. Her flat, white pumps gave an air of middle-class school administrator. Nothing about her appearance suggested menace in any way, shape or form.

So why did Christine feel unsettled?

"Yes, I'm Christine. Nice to meet you."

Freya offered the homemade pie to her. "I brought you a housewarming present."

A delicious whiff of baked apple wafted over her as she accepted the gift. "Thank you."

A sweet smile spread over Freya's face. "Do you like the apples in your garden? I could make cider for you. I did for the family who lived here before you."

Christine gave a forced chortle. "Noah and I might take you up on that. Apple pie for the kids and cider for us."

Freya continued smiling as she fixed Christine with an unbroken stare. "Well, I'll let you get on with things. I just wanted to welcome you to the area."

"Thanks," said Christine. She shut the door without another second to lose.

A few minutes later, the door knocked again. Not Freya back for something else? She stiffened as she went to answer it, but trepidation changed to relief at the outlines of Noah, Emmet and Joely behind the opaque glass.

"Sorry hun, I forgot my key." Noah tapped the side of his head and pulled a face. His grin faded when he looked at her. "What's wrong?"

She shook her head. "Nothing. I was just missing you guys, that's all."

"We met the woman who lives next door, Mum. She seems really nice," said Joely.

"Yeah, she stopped by here as well. She gave us this as a housewarming present." Christine held out the apple pie.

Noah dipped his chin. "Hey, she's not the reason you look so spooked, is she?"

Christine shivered and crossed her arms over her chest. "Maybe."

He laughed. "What, that wee slip of a woman?"

Irritation bubbled up. "Size has nothing to do with it, Noah."

His smile fell. "Okay, okay, it was just a joke. I didn't mean anything by it."

She shook off her bad mood and hugged her husband. "I'm sorry, I didn't mean to be so sharp. I'm sure it's nothing. It's probably because I was home alone in this old place."

"Not exactly, Mum. You were with Jason," Emmet joked. "After all, it's Friday the thirteenth."

She gave him a playful cuff of the ear. "Thanks for reminding me, cheeky sod."

Christine carried the apple pie through to the kitchen. Any reservations she had about Freya were surely silly; it was welcoming and friendly of their neighbour to give them a present. She would serve it up for dessert after dinner. It certainly looked inviting and smelled delicious. Would it be cheeky if she had a quick slice, just to taste? She glanced around for Noah, Joely and Emmet, but they must have gone through to the living room, or the kids in their bedrooms.

Why not? She cut a sliver of pie, a wedge as wide as her finger, and ate it in one bite. Yum. The apple pie was as tasty as it looked; Noah and the kids would be lucky if she didn't devour the whole thing before they even had a piece.

A sudden sleepiness beset her, as if she had eaten a full meal. If she was honest, she could do with a nap. Noah and the kids wouldn't mind if she had a quick forty winks. She made her way out of the kitchen, feeling light-footed, as though her body didn't carry any weight. Strange. The cottage too seemed different somehow, like a veil had dropped over everything. Each room looked like how the bathroom did after a particularly steamy shower, as though the air was shrouded in a fine mist.

Very strange. Very strange indeed.

She turned into her bedroom, her head feeling like a lump of lead on her shoulders, when she noticed that the room wasn't empty.

He was wearing the same grey army-surplus jacket that she had seen him in when he had crossed the garden. Emmet's new friend, Ryan, stood by the window watching her. It was almost as though he had been waiting for her.

"You! Get out of my house. You're trespassing."

He put up both hands. "I'll go. But, please. I need to show you something. It's really important."

She pointed to the door. "I don't think so. Leave now, or I'll phone the police. Stay away from this house and especially from my kids, you hear me? If you ever come near Emmet again, I'll—"

"I know what you're thinking, Christine, but you're getting things wrong. I'm trying to help you. This used to be my house, until last year."

She paused. There was a note of fear, or of panic, or both in his voice that caught her attention.

"You shouldn't be in here. If you kept the key, then you need to give it back to me right now." She held out her open palm.

His frightened expression made him seem much younger than nineteen. He cowered like a child. Christine's heart panged; he didn't seem much older than Emmet all of a sudden.

She softened her tone. "Whatever is so important you can tell me outside."

Ryan nodded. He led her out onto the street. "Thank you. If you don't mind following me to a cottage just two doors along. It'll be really quick, but it's easier if you see it for yourself."

As they approached the front door, it unlocked with a snap, as if a gust of wind had blown it open. What a strange occurrence; and an even crazier coincidence. He stepped inside, although she paused before crossing the threshold. Wasn't it breaking and entering to go inside someone's home without permission?

He seemed to sense her apprehension. "I wouldn't bring you here if it wasn't so important. Please, just take a look, and then you can make up your own mind."

She couldn't say why, but she trusted him. Unlike when Freya had turned up at her doorstep, Christine got no sense of malice from Ryan; even though he had appeared inside her house, rather than at the front door. The layout of the cottage was similar to the inside of her own home. She let him lead her into the kitchen, where he pointed at a laptop that had been left on the counter. As before when the door unlocked by itself, the laptop blinked on in a bright blaze.

A video appeared on the screen showing a view of the kitchen they were in. A red-haired woman wearing a black dress with red hearts knelt beside an unconscious man. Christine recognised the man as Ryan, his head lolling and his eyes closed, but she didn't recognise the red-haired woman. The woman's long tresses obscured her face. All that Christine could see was the dagger she held high above her head, clasped in both hands, as she uttered an incantation to the sky.

"Dark Mother, grant me the immortal soul of this man. Give him to me as my eternal love. Make him subservient to me. Give me this wish and I will worship you and bestow upon your land the gift of his body and his blood to grow new apples."

Christine shrieked as the red-haired woman plunged the dagger into Ryan's chest. Blood spurted upwards, splattering the woman. Although horrified, Christine was unable to peel her eyes away from the laptop screen. The red-haired woman raised her head and finally, she was able to recognise Freya, before she had cut her hair and dyed it blonde.

Freya must have drugged Ryan before she killed him. The video continued to play, and Christine watched as she drained Ryan's blood into a silver chalice. She dipped her finger in it and smeared a heart on the left side of her cleavage, then another in the centre of her forehead. Next, she wrapped his body in a red satin sheet and dragged it into her garden.

A jump cut appeared and a new scene showed Freya's back garden on the screen. With its high fences on three sides, and blocked by two tall apple trees, Christine knew that Freya's crime was hidden from her neighbours. With her Valentine's Day dress now damp with blood, Freya poured Ryan's blood from the silver chalice onto the roots of each apple tree, and then dug a shallow grave between them. She placed his body inside the shallow grave, covered it with soil, and placed three large, terracotta vases on top.

"Dark Mother, send my love to me nightly. Let him visit me, and love me, under the watch of the moon and stars."

Ryan waved his hand in front of the screen, and the video ended. He lowered his head, his eyes downcast.

"Oh Ryan, I'm so sorry," said Christine. "You were murdered. Is that how you were able to come inside my house – you're a ghost?"

He gave a single, solemn nod.

"She killed you last Valentine's Day, didn't she?"

Again, he nodded. "I spend every night with her and then I rest during the day. Do you know the scarecrow in your back garden, the one wearing the grey jacket and the black beanie hat?"

"Yes. It's a horrible, creepy thing."

"That's where she keeps my soul – trapped in the breast pocket. Do you recognise the jacket?" Ryan held wide the lapels of the army surplus jacket he was wearing and Christine gasped. Why hadn't she recognised it sooner?

Her hand flew to her mouth. "Oh my God, are you saying, you were wearing that on the day she murdered you?"

"I'm afraid so. She took it as a keepsake. A kind of morbid trophy, I suppose."

"How did she–" Christine searched for the right words. "I mean, how did it happen?"

"My family moved into your cottage at the start of last year. We didn't know that Freya's father is the landlord. He lets her manage the cottage. If she finds a tenant she's romantically interested in, she rents it out." His voice saddened. "In my case, I became the subject of her affection."

Freya was the landlord's daughter.

"I enrolled at the community college. She turned up in one of my classes and I thought she was beautiful and sophisticated. More mature too. She told me she was twenty-two."

"So you started seeing her?"

"Yes. But apparently that wasn't enough. She wanted more than my body," he said, his voice cracking.

Christine's thoughts churned. "How did she get away with it, though? Your body is in her garden. Didn't your parents wonder where you went?"

Ghostly tears rained down Ryan's cheeks. "Her father, the landlord of the cottage you now rent, is an immigration solicitor. When he found out what Freya did, he helped her to cover up her crime. They pulled strings to get a visa issued for me, saying that I went backpacking with her in South America for a year. My parents knew it was a dream of mine since I was a child – and Freya knew that too. I wasn't particularly close to my parents, sadly. I ran away from home a few times when I was younger, so unfortunately for me, they didn't find that out of character. They actually moved here to make a fresh start and mend their relationship with me, so when they thought I ran off to go and work for a charity helping favela kids, they broke their lease and moved back to Bristol to be near my grandparents."

"Oh Ryan!" Christine opened her arms to him, but then remembered he was a ghost and let her hands drop. "I'm sure they haven't given up looking for you?"

"It seems they have." He lowered his head. "Freya's father has contacts in Brazil. They fabricated a story that I had been killed by a drug cartel. My parents went out there helping to look for my body. They've blown their life savings."

Christine's hands flew to her face. If Freya and her father were so dangerous, what did that mean for her family?

If she finds a tenant she's romantically interested in, she rents it out. What if Noah was her next target? What if she tried to pursue a romantic liaison with him? He would never be interested, Christine trusted him with her life, but that wouldn't stop Freya, would it? Her chest heaved; she was sure Noah was next on Freya's list.

"We had only been out on a few dates when she invited me to her place. I didn't think twice when she gave me some cider that she said she had made from the apple tree out back. It's only now that it's too late, of course, I can see that the cider was drugged."

Christine took a deep breath to steady her rising heartbeat. "Do you think my husband is in danger?"

"I'm *sure* he is. She only rents if there's a man she's attracted to. That's why I showed you this video of Freya's crime."

"Where is she right now?" Christine dashed to the doorway and looked along the hallway of Freya's cottage. No sign of the murderer anywhere in sight.

"She's out getting the things she needs to kill your husband. It's Friday the 13th, a lucky sign for her. She'll be emboldened this year to kill him on Valentine's Day," Ryan warned.

Panic began to rise, in spite of her efforts to stay calm. This was worse than she feared. "I'm going to call the police."

"You can't." Ryan's voice was heavy with sadness.

"But I have to. Your body must still be in her garden, right? All I have to do is get the police to come and dig it up."

He shook his head. "No, it isn't that. You *physically* can't. You're not *in* your body right now."

She blinked at him, confused. "What are you talking about?"

"You ate some of her apple pie. I'm sorry to say you got drugged. You made it as far as your bed before you passed out. It's your soul that I'm talking to right now. Your soul left your body while you fell unconscious. It's called Astral Projection – or you might know it as an Out of Body experience."

Could it be possible? Christine digested his words; he was right. Her first thought after eating the apple pie was that she felt sleepy and everything looked like steam had filtered out after a hot shower. On top of that, she felt light-footed and as she walked around, as though she was weightless.

"I need to get back to my body. I need to wake myself up and warn Noah and the kids."

Ryan's sadness disappeared, replaced by determination. "I'll help you."

They hurried back to her cottage. Ryan was right. Christine saw herself passed out on the bed. She wandered into the kitchen and stopped in her tracks, aghast. Noah, Emmet and Joely were all slumped at the kitchen table. A sizeable chunk had been cut out of the apple pie, and three plates with crumbs lay before each of them.

"They ate some of the pie! They must have seen that I took a slice and helped themselves too," she gasped.

She reached for Noah's shoulders to rouse him, but it was as if her fingertips tried to grab air.

"Ryan, please help. You must know something we can do to wake all of them – all of us," she corrected.

As if in answer to her pleas, the doorbell rang. Both of them drifted to the front door and saw a delivery man through the opaque glass. He was holding two large family-sized pizza boxes.

"Do you think he can see ghosts?" she said.

Ryan shrugged. "We've nothing to lose."

In a blast of wintery air, the front door blew open. Had their combined ghostly presences somehow manifested into psychokinetic energy? She had no time to ponder the notion; it was time to act.

"Excuse me, mister? I don't know if you can see me or not? I need you to come in and help my family – right now," Christine shouted.

The delivery man looked through her and into the hallway. "Hello? Erm, is anyone home? I've got your pizza."

"He can't see me." She threw up her hands, fighting the despair that was welling.

"I'll try. I've been doing this longer than you." Ryan focused his gaze on the man, his eyes narrowed with concentration. "This is an emergency. I need you to find the family inside the kitchen. When you do, call the police."

The delivery man didn't react to Ryan either.

"It's no good. He doesn't have any psychic ability at all, he can't see ghosts."

Just as she was about to sink into despair, the delivery man started to walk inside the cottage. Of course; Noah never paid in advance. He always gave cash on delivery, just to make sure they never got 'ripped off'.

"Hello in there? Did you order pizza? Erm, it'll be forty-eight fifty. I'll bring it through to the kitchen for you and you can pay me there."

"Yes. Please find us. Hurry. Please find us," Christine urged.

The delivery man halted in the kitchen doorway, his jaw hanging low, and surveyed the four unconscious people.

"Oh shit, what's going on?" The pizza delivery man's eyes landed on the partially eaten apple pie and Christine saw the look of confusion spread over his face. He scanned the kitchen, saw fifty pounds that Noah had set aside on the counter for the delivery, grabbed the money and dashed out of the cottage.

"Oh, come on, you've got to be kidding. How could he just leave us here like this?" She threw her hands up in exasperation, but to no avail.

"Hello."

A soft, feminine voice behind made her jump. She spun around to see Freya smiling at her. Since her body was still unconscious in bed, that meant Freya was addressing her spirit self.

"And Ryan, tut tut tut. You should be resting. You'll need your strength for tonight." Freya had a malicious glint in her eye as her smile stretched even further and even more sinister than before. "Of course, the lovely Noah could do instead. Christine, you can blame Ryan if I need to use your husband tonight as my sex slave in place of this naughty boy, roaming free and disobeying me."

"Is that right? Well, I don't think so."

Christine turned to see Noah's spirit arrive from the dining room while his body was still unconscious on the kitchen table. His gaze was steely as he directed his focus on Freya. She had never seen her husband so angry.

"I'll never be your sex slave. I love one woman, and one only, and if you think you can kill me, you have another thing coming."

He pointed to Christine; she couldn't help but smile.

"You won't be smiling when your husband doesn't wake up. Maybe your whole family would like to take a *little trip abroad*?"

Christine's smile faded. Freya was dangerous, and corrupt. If she had used her father's connections to fabricate a visa and trip to Brazil for Ryan, what if she 'disappeared' her whole family. Noah, the kids, and herself too; no trace. It didn't bear thinking about.

No time for fear. Time for action.

"Where are the kids? Are they about?" she asked Noah.

"Their souls – spirits –" He trailed off, lost for words. "They're cowering in the dining room. They're terrified of Freya."

"Then they're smart," said Christine, steeling her voice.

A strange sensation overcame her; a feeling of being tugged by her navel. She followed the invisible pull, which led to her body. The pull became stronger, and she felt herself lifted off her feet and falling forwards, as though off a cliff. She was travelling faster now and sensed air breezing past her face. All of it happened within seconds; then numbness flooded her.

Christine blinked and raised her head up off the bed. She felt sluggish and had a banging headache. Her neck had a from lying face down. She felt like she had the worst hangover in her life.

She staggered into the kitchen, feeling her way along the walls for balance. Noah, Emmet and Joely were still unconscious at the table. She turned her groggy head and saw Freya, frozen in the doorway.

Freya looked like a marionette. Her shoulders were pulled back and her arms held out from her body, as if an invisible person had pinned her under the arms.

Noah's ghost was waiting for her. "There's a man with me called Ryan. He said he used to live here."

"Yes honey, I know. Ryan and I have already met. He was helping me."

"We've got Freya – we're both holding her. Don't ask me how, but we've got her. You need to take your chance. Call the authorities," Noah instructed.

"Right. I'm on it."

Freya squirmed, but was unable to move her body. A callous laugh spluttered from her mouth, sending saliva dribbling down her chin. "You can't blame me for trying. All I ever wanted was a man for Valentine's Day. A man I could love to death."

Any grogginess Christine felt disappeared in a flood of adrenaline. She whipped her phone out of her pocket and dialled 999.

***

The early hours of Valentine's Day weren't how she would have liked the day to start, but at least her family was safe. She cupped her mug in both hands and sipped, allowing comforting warmth to flood over her as she stood on the front doorstep looking down the street. Noah, Emmet and Joely stood on the footpath further along with an assortment of their new neighbours, most of whom they hadn't yet met, but all interested in one thing: the emergency vehicles in front of Freya's cottage.

Freya had been taken to the local police station for questioning. A white tent had been erected in Freya's back garden while forensics in protective suits filed into her cottage. Christine shuddered as an ambulance gurney was wheeled out, knowing that the contents of the black, zipped bag was Ryan's body. An overwhelming sadness engulfed her, until a gentle voice sounded on the breeze behind her and lifted her spirits.

"Don't be sad. You don't know how much you helped me."

Unlike before, she could see through Ryan. He looked more like a ghost and less like a real, solid person.

"But you're fading."

He smiled. "Trust me, that's a good thing. It means my time on earth is over. You found my body. My parents can give me a proper burial."

Christine wiped a tear away. "You were so young, Ryan. You're only a few years older than my Emmet."

He pressed his lips together and shrugged. "Don't be sad. You did an amazing thing by believing me – a ghost – when I needed your help. I can rest now, instead of having to be Freya's plaything."

"You helped me too. You saved my husband from the same fate." She stretched out her arms. "I wish I could hug you."

At that moment, she felt Noah's arm slipping over her shoulder and pulling her in for a hug.

"Both of you saved me." He looked from her to Ryan, smiling at them both. With his other arm, he reached around Ryan's fading form and all three hugged.

"Happy Valentine's Day to you both," said Ryan.

Christine watched him smiling in the moonlight, before he disappeared.

"Happy Valentine's Day to you too, Ryan. May you rest in peace."

OTHER BOOKS BY
LEILANIE STEWART

Diabolical Dreamscapes: Strange and macabre short stories

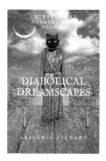

Reader beware! From the hallucinatory imagination of Leilanie Stewart, author of award-winning ghost horror novel, The Blue Man, comes twenty-one previously published short stories and flash fiction, now entombed between the covers of a new darkly themed collection.

In Part 1: Dark and Surreal Tales of Death: Corpses find new purposes in death while fated to walk the earth and surreal journeys of the afterlife abound, involving trips to far-reaching corners of the earth, the moon, or Venus during the last throes of life.

In Part 2: Strange and Hallucinatory Stories of the Mind: Cats, rabbits, dogs, birds and spiders have a role to play in these dreamlike journeys through the mind, helping the characters of each tale unravel their fears and anxiety, while facing their darkness, depression and demons.

Pseudologia Fantastica: Four stories of stalkers and mythomaniacs

Envy. Lust. Control.
Power.

How far would a person go in their obsessive quest of another? In these two short stories and two novellas, ordinary people, going about their everyday lives, become the playthings of fantasists, who shape the narrative to achieve their ultimate goal: total domination over their targets.

Will their innocent victims realise the dysfunctional game they are unwittingly a part of, before it is too late?

The Blue Man: A haunted friendship across the decades

Belfast Ghosts – Standalone Book 1 of 3

Chill with a Book Premier Readers' Award and Book of the Month winner, February 2023

Two best friends. An urban legend. A sinister curse.

Twenty years ago, horror loving Sabrina told her best friend, Megan, the terrifying Irish folk tale of the Blue Man, who sold his soul to the Devil in vengeance against a personal injustice. What should have been the best summer of their schooldays turned into a waking nightmare, as the Blue Man came to haunt Megan. Sabrina, helpless to save Megan from a path of self-destruction and substance abuse as she sought refuge from the terror, left Belfast for a new life in Liverpool.

Twenty years later, the former friends reunited thinking they had escaped the horrors of the past. Both were pregnant for the first time. Both had lived elsewhere and moved back to their hometown, Belfast. Both were wrong about the sinister reality of the Blue Man, as the trauma of their school days caught up to them – and their families.

Why did the Blue Man terrorise Megan? Was there more to the man behind the urban legend? Was their friendship – and mental health – strong enough to overcome a twenty year curse?

The Fairy Lights: The ghost of Christmas that never was

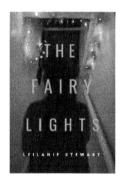

Belfast Ghosts – Standalone Book 2 of 3

Author Shout Reader Ready Awards – Recommended Read 2024 winner

When Aisling moves into an old, Edwardian house in the university area of Stranmillis, Belfast, she soon discovers that her student digs are haunted. The house, bought by her grandfather decades ago, is also home to a spirit known by the nickname Jimbo.

As yuletide approaches, and Aisling's Christmas fairy lights attract mischief from Jimbo, she seeks to find out more about the restless entity. With the help of a local psychic and friends from her History with Irish course, Aisling uncovers dark, buried truths. What is the connection with Friar's Bush Graveyard just around the corner? What does Jimbo's dusty book of the Oak King and Holly King, hidden in the attic, have to reveal? What will Aisling's journey into the darkness of the spirit world reveal about Jimbo – and herself?

Matthew's Twin: The spirit of medieval vengeance made flesh

Belfast Ghosts – Standalone Book 3 of 3

A medieval Scottish soldier.
An Anglo-Irish witch.
A seven hundred year plot for revenge.

Around the time Customs Inspector Matthew began having crippling stomach pains, he began witnessing visions of a past-life involving a Scottish soldier during Edward Bruce's conquest of Ireland, an Anglo-Irish defender of Carrickfergus Castle and a local witch with a bloodthirsty agenda. When medieval mercenary and vengeful witch performed a necromantic ritual to help the Scottish conquest succeed, Matthew began to learn more about his connection with 14th century Northern Ireland.

After an operation to remove what he thought to be a tumour from his stomach, a mysterious man arrived to cause chaos in Matthew's life. What did the strange – yet familiar – man have to do with him? Why did malign forces from a dark, medieval past want to cause harm? Was there any way for Matthew to learn about a seven hundred year injustice before the ghosts came to wreak vengeance on him in the present?

Gods of Avalon Road

London, present day.
Kerry Teare and her university friend Gavin move to London to work for the enigmatic Oliver Doncaster.

Their devious new employer lures them into an arcane occult ritual involving a Golden Horse idol.

Britannia, AD 47.
Aithne is the Barbarian Queen of the Tameses tribes. The Golden Warrior King she loves is known as Belenus. But are the mutterings of the Druids true: is he really the Celtic Sun God himself?

Worlds collide as Oliver's pagan ritual on Mayday summons gods from the Celtic Otherworld of Avalon. Kerry is forced to confront the supernatural deities and corrupt mortals trying to control her life and threatening her very existence.

The Buddha's Bone: A dark psychological journey to find light

She was in Japan to teach English. She'd soon discover the darker side of travelling alone.

Death
Kimberly Thatcher wasn't an English teacher. She wasn't a poet. She wasn't an adventurer. Now she wasn't even a fiancée. But when one of her fellow non-Japanese colleagues tried to make her a victim, she said no.

Cremation
In Japan on a one-year teaching contract at a private English language school, and with her troubled relationship far behind her in London, Kimberly set out to make new friends. She would soon discover the darker side of travelling alone – and people's true intentions.

Rebirth
As she came to question the nature of all those around her – and herself – Kimberly was forced to embark on a soul-searching journey into emptiness. What came next after you looked into the abyss? Could Kimberly overcome the trauma – of sexual assault and pregnancy loss – blocking her path to personal enlightenment along the way, and forge a new identity in a journey of–

Death. Cremation. Rebirth.

ABOUT THE AUTHOR

Leilanie Stewart is an award-winning author and poet from Belfast, Northern Ireland. She writes ghost and psychological horror, as well as experimental verse. Her writing confronts the nature of self; her novels feature main characters on a dark psychological journey who have a crisis and create a new sense of identity. She began writing for publication while working as an English teacher in Japan, a career pathway that has influenced themes in her writing. Her former career as an Archaeologist has also inspired her writing and she has incorporated elements of archaeology and mythology into both her fiction and poetry.

In addition to promoting her own work, Leilanie teaches creative writing to sixth form students and works in a library, where she indulges her passion of books.

Aside from literary pursuits, Leilanie enjoys spending time with her author husband, Joseph Robert, and their lively literary lad, a voracious reader of sea monster books.

www.leilaniestewart.com

Acknowledgements

Where would I be without my super hubby and editor, Joseph Robert? Thank you for all the fabulous editing and polish and also your feedback on the graphic design of the cover. Happy Valentine's Day, love you!

Thanks to my lovely ARC readers, Jeanne Bertille and Nathan McKee, as well as the book bloggers who support my work: Laura at the Bookish Hermit and Hannah at Hannah May Book reviews.

And, many thanks to you for buying my book. Having readers keeps me motivated to write more stories, so just to let you know that I appreciate you taking the time to read and review my books. It means more than you know.

Printed in Great Britain
by Amazon